L.M.

"I told you, Kendra, first one up buys breakfast," Mac insisted.

"What time is it?" she asked.

"Close to nine," he told her.

"Breakfast is served until ten-thirty."

"We need time to freshen up, Kendra." He moved from the closet to the couch and dropped down beside her. "Frankly, darlin', I think it may take you a while."

Her mouth dropped open, but instead of the protest she intended to register, laughter bubbled out. She could tell he was pleased with her reaction from the twinkle in his eye. "You're outrageous," she said.

"No, ma'am. I'm a little outlandish, maybe. Outstanding, definitely. Out to lunch, sometimes. But outrageous?" He touched his finger to the tip of her nose. "Outrageous is the way you look good enough to eat first thing in the morning. Outrageous is having a mouth that just begs for long, deep kisses." He drew back and studied her blushing face. "Outrageous is your not knowing just how hungry you make me. . . ."

WHAT ARE *LOVESWEPT* ROMANCES?

They are stories of true romance and touching emotion. We believe those two very important ingredients are constants in our highly sensual and very believable stories in the *LOVESWEPT* line. Our goal is to give you, the reader, stories of consistently high quality that may sometimes make you laugh, sometimes make you cry, but are always fresh and creative and contain many delightful surprises within their pages.

Most romance fans read an enormous number of books. Those they truly love, they keep. Others may be traded with friends and soon forgotten. We hope that each *LOVESWEPT* romance will be a treasure—a "keeper." We will always try to publish

LOVE STORIES YOU'LL NEVER FORGET
BY AUTHORS YOU'LL ALWAYS REMEMBER

The Editors

Loveswept ® 544

Joyce Anglin
Old Devil Moon

BANTAM BOOKS

NEW YORK · TORONTO · LONDON · SYDNEY · AUCKLAND

OLD DEVIL MOON

A Bantam Book / May 1992

*If you would be interested in receiving protective vinyl
covers for your Loveswept books, please write to this address
for information:*

> Loveswept
> Bantam Books
> P.O. Box 985
> Hicksville, NY 11802

ISBN 0-553-44201-5

Published simultaneously in the United States and Canada

Bantam Books are published by Bantam Books, a division of
Bantam Doubleday Dell Publishing Group, Inc. Its trademark,
consisting of the words "Bantam Books" and the portrayal of
a rooster, is Registered in U.S. Patent and Trademark Office
and in other countries. Marca Registrada. Bantam Books, 666
Fifth Avenue, New York, New York 10103.

PRINTED IN THE UNITED STATES OF AMERICA

OPM   0 9 8 7 6 5 4 3 2 1

One

"It won't be so bad. It won't be so bad. It won't be so—"

A resounding thud, accompanied by hoots and rebel yells, interrupted the mantra Kendra Davis had been chanting for the better part of an hour. It was at least the tenth wall-shaking thud since the first one that had awakened her, and it was the last she intended to endure.

"You were wrong, Leslie," she grumbled to her absent friend as she poked her head, then her shoulders, and finally her arms from beneath the mound of blankets and quilts covering her hotel bed. "It *is* bad."

"Colorado cold is different," Leslie had assured her. "Drier. You'll hardly notice it." Hah! Not even several blankets and quilts could effectively counter the chill in her supposedly deluxe room. It was colder than a witch's—well, it was cold. "Never, never will I listen to you again," Kendra muttered, thinking of all the ways she would repay her best friend, if and when Leslie ever showed up at the "quaint" ski lodge. Obviously, *quaint* had a different definition in travel brochures than it did in a dictionary.

With a tired sigh, Kendra reached for the telephone. A shiver chased through her as she tucked the frigid receiver against her ear and punched the by now familiar number.

"Front desk," a fuzzy voice announced.

"This is room two-twelve. I need to speak to security, please."

"You got *another* problem?" The nasal voice at the other end of the line sounded almost as enthused as it had when Kendra had called for extra blankets and then again to check on the progress of the heating repairs.

"What I've got," Kendra said, "is a party next door."

"Oh, yeah?"

At last, Kendra thought. She'd sparked some interest.

"You mean those guys from Atlanta?"

"I mean those guys who have been banging against the walls all night. Could you send security to quiet them down?"

"Sorry, security is on rounds."

Kendra dredged up the last ounce of forbearance remaining in her weary body. "Well, can't you page them? Surely they carry beepers."

"Oh, yeah. *He* does. Only it isn't working so good."

Just like the heat. Just like the vacation. Just like the last two months of her life. And she'd actually thought getting away might help her see her problems with more objectivity. "Never mind," she told the front desk, dragging a hand over her sleep hungry eyes. "I'll take care of it."

It took another thud before she scrounged enough energy to climb from under the patchwork covers. When her stockinged feet touched the floor she let out a small sigh of relief. It was getting warmer. The cold no longer leeched through her argyle socks like ice water. She puffed out a long breath. She couldn't see it anymore. Things were looking up. She was on a roll.

It lasted until she rapped on the door of the neighboring room. As soon as a brown-eyed hunk with a shock of wheat-colored hair answered her knock, her exhilaration started a downhill slide. He ran his gaze from her down-filled coat to the hem of her flannel nightgown and two dimples appeared on either side of his mouth along with a lazy grin. Oh, great, she thought. Adonis meets the bag lady.

She squared her shoulders and forced herself to hold his gaze. A mistake. The sparkling warmth in his eyes sent heat surging through her chilled limbs.

It's not because of him, she told herself. It can't be. She knew better than to get all soppy over some guy's good looks. It must be fatigue or—she pressed her hand to her forehead—fever. But it was definitely not him.

"Hey, darlin'." The hunk propped his shoulder against the door frame with insouciant ease. "You come to join our little party?"

His honey-thick drawl kindled a ridiculous curl of warmth in the pit of her stomach.

"I came to ask you to hold the party down," she said, wondering what the chances were she was having some sort of premenopausal hot flash. "Or better yet, call the party off." She punctuated her last request with a trumped-up smile as she watched perspiration bead up near his temple and trickle down his cheek. It was quite possibly the sexiest trickle she'd ever seen.

Get a grip, Kendra. It's sweat, for heaven's sake!

She forced her attention back to his eyes. "I'd really like to get some sleep tonight."

"That could be arranged."

When his gaze strayed to the open collar of her zippered coat, astonishment mingled with another surge of heated awareness. If she'd been a voluptuous woman with cotton-candy hair in a see-through nightie, she might—possibly—have understood the gleam of invitation in his chocolate-brown eyes. But she wasn't voluptuous, the ruffled neckline of her nightgown was a mile shy of provocative, and her uncombed hair couldn't remind anyone of anything delectable. Obviously, the man was an indiscriminate wolf, pure and simple.

"I'd appreciate your cooperation," she said, trying to ignore the sensual current that flowed from him like lava. As she turned to leave, a thud echoed from inside the room.

"Come on Mac!" called another drawling voice. "Jennings is gonna score again if you don't get in here and block."

Kendra stopped in midstride. "Football?" she asked, stunned with disbelief.

Mac shrugged. "Just a little block and tackle." He smiled. "It's a big room."

"And you're a big guy," she said, shaking her head. "You should save your games for the great outdoors."

"Yes, ma'am." His smile tilted a little. "Sorry we disturbed you. We thought the rest of the floor was empty on account of the heat not working."

"The heat is working now."

"Is it?" He cocked his head. "Kind of hard to tell, it's so chilly out here."

She felt the sting of his barbed comment all the way back to her room. She unlocked her door, wondering for a moment what it would be like to be less reserved, to be able to smile and flirt with a macho hunk, as if it were the greatest thing since eating peanut butter. But she'd spent too many years fighting to drop her guard easily. Smiles and charm hadn't gotten her a medical degree. Determination, and self-reliance were her allies, even if they sometimes proved to be poor companions.

She crawled back into bed, dismayed that one little encounter could cause her to doubt herself. She couldn't afford to add another straw to the growing pile on the proverbial camel's back. So what if Mac was gorgeous? He was only a man. She punched her pillow. A gorgeous man was the last thing she needed in her life right now.

She fell asleep smoothing out the pillow and awoke with it cradled in her arms. A glance at the clock told her it was too early to get up, but sleep was now impossible. Sunlight cut like a laser through a permanent gap in the draperies covering the sliding glass door to her balcony.

This wasn't how her first vacation was supposed to be, Kendra thought grumpily, burying her head under the covers. What happened to sleeping till noon? What happened to rest, rest, and more rest? A burst of laughter from the next room nudged through her cocoon of blankets. That was it. She surrendered. She should have known; if the sun couldn't get her, something else would.

She dressed quickly for breakfast, looking forward to a peaceful meal and a chance to see Colorado in the clear light of day. However, no sooner was she seated at a small table covered with a faded yellow cloth than Mac and his football buddies trooped in.

The late hours hadn't seemed to do Mac any harm, Kendra noted, taking in the square set of his shoulders, the clean line of his jaw. His eyes danced with humor, showing no trace of the weariness that rimmed hers. His gaze was sharp and clear and—oh, Lord—aimed straight at her. She glanced away, but not quickly enough to miss his nod of acknowledgment. Darn! Now he probably thought she was ogling him. And, she realized, he wouldn't be far off the mark.

She buried her head in her menu, hoping she didn't appear as flushed as she felt.

Her waitress whisked up to the table.

"So, hon, what'll it be?" The woman's gum cracked rhythmically while Kendra glanced over the hand-printed list of morning specials.

"Number three, please," she said, picking

scrambled eggs and hash browns. To heck with cholesterol. She was going to enjoy something while she was on vacation, even if it was only the foods she fastidiously avoided at home. "With sausage patties instead of links. And could I have toast instead of pancakes?" A tiny concession for fractionally less fat.

"Sorry," the waitress said with another sharp pop of her gum. "No substitutions."

"Oh . . . well." Kendra scanned the menu again.

"Look, why don't you take another minute to decide while I wait on the next table?"

Before Kendra could say another word, the brassy blonde was gone. Peeved, Kendra watched her sashay over to the next table. Mac's table.

Figures, she thought, watching the woman flash a smile almost as big as her pushed up bosom. There was nothing like a good-looking man to make *some* women turn on like a light bulb.

"Okay, fellas," the waitress cooed. "What can I get you?"

Coffee was the unanimous request.

"Sure thing." As she leaned across the table to distribute menus, her impressive chest hovered at eye level over the napkin holder. "You just take a look at these while I go get it."

With a wink, she was gone, expertly avoiding Kendra's attempt to capture her attention. Five minutes later Kendra was still waiting, while Mac was taking his first sip of the steaming hot brew she'd yet to have.

"You fellas hang on now," the waitress said as

she placed the last cup before a man who looked to be a preserved fifty. "I'll be right back, soon as I take care of the little gal over there."

Little gal? Kendra looked over her shoulder. Then she realized *she* was the little gal—and that the masculine chuckle she heard was Mac's.

With steely resolve, Kendra kept herself from glaring at either the waitress or Mac. She was not going to let something so petty eat at her. She was here to relax, to enjoy, to cleanse herself, as Leslie put it, from the need to right every wrong, to heal every wound, and to pave the road to a better life for her younger sister, Bridgett.

Resolutely, she welcomed the waitress with a calm smile. She managed to give her order in a pleasant tone, even when told grapefruit juice wasn't on the menu and she had to settle for tomato. She was going to remain calm for the rest of the day. That was her goal—to smile, relax, enjoy.

"Anything else, hon?"

Kendra was determined not to let the "hon" get to her.

"That should do it. Thanks."

"Sure thing, hon. It'll be out in a few minutes." She swished back to Mac's table to take orders.

Kendra tried not to listen to the laughing banter. It was none of her business if Mr. Fifty and Fabulous thought "Sugar," as he called the waitress, should join them for an afternoon on the slopes. It was none of her concern if "Sugar's" knack for being breezy and cheerful won the sort of instant approval Kendra had never been able to earn.

When "Sugar" pulled herself away from Mac and Fred, Arthur, Skip, and Terry, to bring her breakfast, Kendra finally began to relax and enjoy herself. The food was exceptionally good, the view of the Rockies from the dining room window breathtaking. Leslie had been right about one thing: No problem could seem as large when held up to the majestic grandeur of these rugged timeless mountains.

"Some hot coffee to top you off?" "Sugar" asked when Kendra had finished.

"No, thank you." Kendra gave the woman a genuine smile. "I'll just take the check, please."

"It's been taken care of, hon."

"I beg your pardon?"

"You got an admirer, doll. And a mighty good lookin' one at that. He picked up the tab." She winked and cracked her gum in one well timed motion. "Gave me a nice little tip too."

"But I—I—"

"Now, hon, it's no big deal."

"It is to me. I'm not in the habit of letting strangers pay my bills." Kendra's tone was as tight as her suddenly knotted stomach.

"Well, I don't think he meant it as any more than a friendly gesture. Folks get to be real friendly up here, you know."

"That's not the point."

"Is there a problem, ma'am?" The low, sexy drawl came from close beside her. She'd been so unsettled, she hadn't seen Mac approach her table.

Embarrassment flooded her. She hadn't intended to create a scene, and certainly not one big enough to draw his attention. But before she could dismiss his question, the waitress jumped in. With both feet.

"She doesn't let strangers pay her bills."

Mac's smile was as slow and easy as his voice. "Well, now, that's good to know. But I'm no stranger, darlin'. Don't you remember? We met last night. You had on that little nightie with the lace up around your throat."

Heat swept up Kendra's cheeks as interest leaped into the waitress's eyes. The knot in Kendra's stomach swelled to the size of a noose—a noose she would have liked to drop over Mac's handsome head. "I'm aware of when and how we met, Mr. . . . ?"

"O'Conner. MacKenzie O'Conner."

"Mr. O'Conner. Look, I'm not trying to be unreasonable, but I really cannot allow you to pay for my meal. I—"

"I know. You don't allow strangers to pay for you, but we've already covered that." He gave her one of his dimpled smiles. "Besides, I felt it was the least I can do, what with keeping you awake half the night."

Kendra could have sworn the waitress was going to pull up a chair and sit down.

Mac obviously thought the same. "Sugar, would you be kind enough to get me another cup of coffee? And one for the lady, too. I think we need another minute or two to hash this out."

Kendra didn't know whether to thank him for getting rid of the eavesdropper, or to kick him when he casually slid his six-foot plus frame into the chair across from her. She chose the middle ground, addressing one of her pet peeves.

"Haven't you ever heard of names?" she asked. "Hers isn't Sugar, and mine isn't Darlin'."

"Yes, it is."

"I—What?"

"That's her name. Sugar. It's right there on her name tag. Unfortunately, darlin', you don't wear one."

His voice wrapped around his words like well-worn suede, cushioning them with a blanket of sensuality. Kendra stared into his sparkling brown eyes and felt her hostility weaken. She was handling this badly, she knew, but flirtatious banter had never been one of her fortes. Especially not with an attractive man whose muscles filled out a plaid flannel shirt so nicely, whose eyes twinkled with humor and masculine interest, whose face could redefine handsome. Never had she felt quite so inadequate. She could handle a crisis with all the skills of a well-trained professional; she could make life-and-death decisions without a second thought. But she could not deal with this. She didn't know how. She'd never had time for things like . . . this before.

"Again, Mr. O'Conner, I appreciate your—"

"Make it Mac."

"Fine. Mac. I appreciate your gesture, but I'm quite capable of paying for my own breakfast. And I've always found it best not to accept favors before I know what's expected in return. You do understand, don't you?"

"Not really." Though sensuality still laced his voice, censure now sharpened his tone. "I've never considered good manners a favor. And I don't collect on favors when I give them. Treating you to breakfast was a form of apology for last night. Nothing more."

She felt like a louse. She'd been close-minded and judgmental, traits neither her profession nor her conscience could tolerate.

"All right then, Mac. I accept your apology and your generosity." The words were difficult for her to say. Even more difficult was offering a smile. "I'm afraid I'm a little testy from my trip. Must be jet lag."

He quirked his brows and cocked his head.

"St. Louis," she informed him.

His low chuckle slipped straight through her defenses.

"I know, I know," she conceded. "It's not across an ocean. But the flight seemed to have taken forever because of the horrible weather."

"You came in last night?"

She nodded. His question surprised her. She'd assumed he'd know the exact moment any eligible female arrived at the lodge, down to the second. Another judgment. She'd taken one look at him and figured he'd surveyed every woman in the hotel with the same thorough perusal he'd given her. And with the same invitation in his eyes.

"I guess that's why you got stuck on the second floor with us," he said.

This time she was puzzled.

"We got in about six, after they'd already moved most of the guests to others floors. We kind of like to keep our rooms within shouting distance of each other, and they'd have had to spread us all over the lodge if we weren't willing to take a chance on the heating getting fixed. Anyway"—he shrugged his broad shoulders—"no sense letting a little heating problem spoil our fun."

"Heaven forbid," she said drolly.

He gave her a rueful grin. "Yes, ma'am, I take my fun seriously."

"Strictly a good-time guy, huh?" She could already see the answer in his laughing eyes.

"That's one way of lookin' at it. I—"

"Well, I see you two have mended your fences," Sugar interrupted, setting two steaming coffee mugs on the table. She gave Kendra a knowing smile. "Hard to stay mad at a good-looking man, isn't it, hon?"

"At times." Kendra tried not to roll her eyes. Sugar didn't know at what a low premium she prized looks.

"Don't kid yourself, Sugar. She had me on my knees." Mac gave the waitress a devilish grin. His dimples slashed his cheeks with rakish appeal.

"Oh, go on now. You're a sweeper, Mac. Right off her feet."

That was probably dead center, Kendra thought, watching Sugar preen under Mac's widening smile. Men who could charm as easily as he rarely had to ask for anything. But she'd been on the receiving end of too much empty charm not to know it wasn't an accurate barometer of character. Her own father had taught her that painful lesson.

She shifted in her chair, fighting the tension that thoughts of her family always evoked.

"You folks drink up now, hear?" Sugar nodded

toward their coffee. "Need to get nice and warm from the inside out before you hit the slopes."

"Will do," Mac promised.

With a satisfied smile, Sugar sashayed off to another table.

"I think your friends are leaving," Kendra said, noticing one of the men putting a tip beside his empty plate.

Mac shrugged. Clearly he had no intention of racing after them, as she'd hoped. The tension she was fighting grew stronger.

"Well," she said, striving to sound firm yet friendly, "I'd better get back to my room now. I have a call to make."

"You wouldn't want to make a liar out of me, would you . . . *darlin'*." Mac's gaze flicked to the coffee. "Sugar might lose her high opinion of me and we wouldn't want that, would we . . . *darlin'*?"

She gave him a grudging smile. "Kendra Davis."

"There, that wasn't so bad, was it?"

"I'm not sure. Am I bleeding?"

"Nary a drop." His brown eyes twinkled for a moment before settling into a look of curiosity. "And I just have to know. Where's your ring?"

"My ring?"

"The one that tells a man straight out a woman's not available.

"I'm not married."

"Engaged? Or involved?"

"No!" she said in mild exasperation at his rapid-fire inquisition.

"Good." His smile spread like sunshine. "Since

we're both free agents, there's no reason you can't meet me on the slopes this afternoon."

Kendra's gaze moved from the warmth of his smile to the snow-covered peaks outside the restaurant windows. Already, daring skiers were traversing the trails, moving in graceful sweeps like athletic dancers. Their skill impressed her; their abandon intimidated her. She could just see Mac skimming over the snow with practiced ease, her bumping along on her rear end or buried neck-deep in a snowdrift.

"No, thank you," she said. Making a complete fool out of herself wasn't a prospect she relished.

"No to the skiing, or no to me?"

"Are the two separate?" she asked sweetly. As soon as the words were out, she realized she'd made him sound like a worthless ski bum. She glanced warily at the rigid set of his jaw, the only outward indication her comment had touched his temper.

"I see," he drawled softly. "Then if you'll excuse me, *Kendra*, I'll go catch up with my friends." He stood, pausing only to slide his chair back under the table. "Enjoy your day. And don't worry, we won't disturb your sleep tonight."

She'd been right. MacKenzie O'Conner skied like a man born to the sport. Aggressive, strong, smooth, he flowed down the mountainside, schussing near the fall line in a last flight to the bottom. Kendra watched until his neon-bright multicolored vest disappeared behind a stand of firs.

"Fabulous, isn't it?" Marcia, the ski instructor Kendra was working with, nodded toward the advanced skier's hill.

"Intimidating."

"All you need is practice and confidence," the woman advised. Her white teeth flashed in an encouraging smile. "You'll get there. And you'll love it."

Kendra shook her head. "Maybe in my next life."

"Oh, come on! You're doing great for a beginner."

"The six-year-olds are doing better," Kendra complained. Proof of her statement went gliding by, tucking their small bodies in close to their knees. Straight as little arrows, right down the bunny slope.

Marcia laughed. "They have an advantage. They're closer to the ground, so they're not as afraid of falling."

"By now, I shouldn't be either. If there's an award for the most tumbles in one day, we both know I win hands down."

"But it's happening less and less often."

An hour later, after falling only twice more, Kendra decided to call it a day. She was exhausted but exuberant, her legs shaking with fatigue, muscles accustomed to aerobic workouts screaming in agony.

"Okay, gang," Marcia called to Kendra and her fellow beginners, "be sure to hit the hot tubs tonight. Your bodies will thank you for it, and you'll be ready to start again bright and early in the morning. First session is at nine."

As Kendra stamped her feet to release her bindings, she tried not to look for Mac, but she found herself daring glances toward the run she'd seen him take earlier.

"Oh, my God!" The panicked cry snapped Kendra's attention back to the slope. A loose ski was tumbling down the hill like a runaway train. And directly in its path was MacKenzie O'Conner. Kendra's heart banged in alarm when the ski hit Mac with a force that felled him like dead weight.

Pulling out of her stunned daze, Kendra scanned the mountain, searching for the ski patrol.

Two uniformed figures were already making their way toward Mac.

"Where will they take him?" she asked Marcia.

"First aid is right over there." She pointed.

Kendra spun, only to be stopped short by a restraining hand. "You might get in the way," Marcia said gently.

"I'm a doctor," Kendra said. And she took off toward the first-aid station, telling herself she was only doing what any doctor would do.

Two

Kendra glanced around her room and shifted restlessly on the bed. Her thoughts kept jumping like water droplets on a hot skillet and MacKenzie O'Connor appeared to be their favorite resting place.

A mild concussion wasn't so bad, she reminded herself for the hundredth—or was it the thousandth?—time. Mac would recover. He was actually pretty darn lucky. So why couldn't she get him off her mind?

He wasn't her type. At all. She'd been assured of that in the first aid station. His friends, Skip and Terry, had been a mine of information about "good ol' Mac."

"Remember when we all decided to run on down to Dallas one weekend, and that woman Mac had been seein' followed him. Man, oh, man." Terry or Skip, which ever had been telling the story, had laughed and slapped his thigh.

"Yeah," his companion had agreed, chuckling. "I can't remember the last time I've seen a female so het up. Lordy, remember the look on Mac's face when she'd showed up?"

"And then there was the time we took off for Florida . . ."

The men had continued sharing stories and laughter, but Kendra had not been amused. She'd gotten a quick insight into Mac's lifestyle: take a notion, take a flight. No, he was definitely not her type at all.

She turned the book she'd been trying to read facedown on her nightstand, and stifled a moan when her arm muscles protested the small action. She'd bet Mac's muscles didn't get that sore from skiing. He probably worked out every day. After all, you didn't get muscles like his— Damn! She was doing it again.

Relentlessly, she pushed him to the rear of her thoughts and reached for the telephone. Leslie answered on the third ring, the sound of her voice as welcome and reassuring as a warm hug. But the news that she couldn't make it to Colorado was not.

"It's all right, Leslie," Kendra lied. It wasn't all right. It was the pits.

"I'm really sorry," Leslie said. "But the girl is at a crisis point, and if I leave now, well, frankly I don't know what she might do."

Kendra sighed and sank down into the pillows. She ran her hand over the blue and mauve quilt, waiting for her disappointment to subside. Understanding Leslie's predicament didn't make it any easier to face a longer stretch of solitude.

"Maybe I should just come home," she said half to herself, half to Leslie.

"Why? Aren't you having a good time?"

"Oh, sure," Kendra said dryly. "When I got here, the heating system on this floor was out and I half froze. Then some aging delinquents decided to play football all night in the room next door. That was a real treat."

"Hey, it has to beat cruising the E.R. and waiting for the next accident victim to roll in." It was never a long wait in St. Louis's largest hospital, where the two friends worked.

"I've gotten my share of that too." She pulled the quilt up over her feet. As Kendra described Mac's accident, twilight shadows darkened the room and cast the mountains beyond her balcony into intimidating austerity.

"Sounds like you couldn't resist playing doctor," Leslie chided after Kendra told her about following Mac to the first aid station. "You're supposed to be on a vacation, remember?"

"I just wanted to make sure he was all right."

"Oh?" Leslie's tone held speculation. "And what does he look like?"

Kendra almost lied, just to keep Leslie from making mountains out of molehills. But she couldn't make herself do it. "He's gorgeous."

"Is that interest I hear in your voice? I can't believe it's working already."

"What is?"

"Zi vacation, dahlink. Zi R and R. Ve zyciatrists haf veys of making patients better by oh so subtle, but effective means."

"Okay, doctor, what are you getting at?"

"You've actually noticed a man as something other than a condition or a case number. That's progress, my dear."

"I thought my objective here was to get away from problems, not cultivate them."

"So you admit you consider men a problem."

"That's not true!" Kendra insisted, kicking off the covers in a sudden wave of heat. True, she didn't make men a priority in her life, but she had valid reasons and Leslie knew that.

"Now, don't get defensive on me. I just want you to relax and enjoy yourself."

Kendra sighed out her irritation. "I know. And I know this vacation is long overdue and well deserved—you've reminded me often enough. I just think I should be home, confronting things instead of running away."

"You're not running away. I'd be the first to tell you if that were true—you know that. But I honestly believe this is best. For you and Bridgett."

"Have you heard from her?" Kendra asked quietly.

"Now why would *I* be hearing from *your* little sister?"

"I don't know. I'm grasping at straws. But I left word that if she needed anything—"

"All she needs is some space."

"Then she should have stayed in college," Kendra argued. "She was free as a bird there."

"Kendra—"

"I know, I know." She climbed from the bed and paced to the window, carrying the telephone. "She's not a child anymore," Kendra dutifully repeated. "But she always used to confide in me. What happened?"

Leslie's silence was as loud as the questions rolling around in Kendra's head. There weren't any answers. Not yet. But she hoped that if she and Bridgett could quit bickering long enough, the lines of communication would open up again, and they could sort things out.

"So, I guess I'm on my own until you work your miracle with your client," Kendra said on another sigh.

"I think you'll survive."

"If I don't, I'm coming back to haunt you."

Leslie's laugh was welcome. "If you come back, I expect you to haunt the chief of staff. He's the one who deserves it."

Kendra laughed with her. "I'll think about it," she promised. "And I'll call you in a couple of days if I haven't heard from you before then."

After she'd said good-bye to Leslie, the walls started closing in again. Nothing on television looked good; her book wasn't holding her attention. She was restless and a little hungry. Surely her concern about Mac had nothing to do with her restlessness. She'd just go down to the restaurant and have dinner. Then she could relax with a nice full tummy in a nice warm bed on a cold, empty night.

Stop it, Kendra! A few days alone were not going to kill her. She'd been alone before. Bridgett had been away at college for over a year before she'd decided to drop out, coming home only for the summer and for Christmas and Easter breaks.

And Kendra always had work. Here, however, all she had was time.

She slipped a cable-knit sweater over her teal blouse and headed for the elevator. Her stomach rumbled grumpily, admonishing her for skipping lunch. But a nap had felt mandatory after her workout on the slopes.

When she passed Mac's room, she almost knocked to see if he or the friend sitting with him needed anything. But she'd already played doctor—and a mother hen today. Reminding herself she was on vacation, she breezed down to the restaurant.

Nightlife at a ski lodge wasn't as decadent as she'd heard. Oh, there were people in the great room, sitting around the fire, laughing and talking, but there was no loud music, no wild dancing or incipient orgy. In fact, it was so sedate she was a little disappointed.

Then she saw the "boys."

Sitting in a conversation pit near a second, smaller fireplace, Skip, Arthur, Terry, and Fred seemed to be having a grand old time. The low-backed, leather couch cushioned two women holding court over the mesmerized quartet. And if the hoots erupting from the pit were any indication, the young women were ace comediennes going through their hilarious repertoire.

Unimpressed, Kendra headed for the restaurant. Then she stopped cold, realizing that if Terry, Skip, Fred, and Arthur were all *here*, no one was with Mac. Anger throbbed within her. She turned, ready to launch an attack.

"Well, hi there, little lady," one of the men called

to her as she approached. "Come on over and have a seat." He patted an empty spot on the couch. "Lilly, honey, scooch on over and make room for . . ."

"Kendra Davis," she supplied.

"That's right, that's right." He beamed at her as if she'd managed a great feat by knowing her own name.

"Actually, I just came to ask about Mac. I take it he's doing okay?"

The man blinked stupidly, then darted his gaze toward the others.

"Why, he's doing just fine," Mr. Fifty-and-Fabulous assured her. "You checked on him last, didn't you, Skip? He was doing fine, wasn't he?"

Skip looked blank. "Well . . . sure . . . he was fine last time I saw him." He smiled and rubbed his chin. "Sleeping like a log. Right, Arthur?"

"Like a log," Arthur agreed.

Irritation surged in her, swift and hot. "When was the last time you looked in on him?" She kept her tone polite, professional.

"Oh, 'bout one . . . two o'clock maybe."

Kendra glanced at her watch. Seven o'clock. Five, maybe six, hours without checking him for lucidity, much less consciousness.

"Don't you think one of you should go up and see if he needs anything?"

Arthur looked at her, then at the twenty-year-old beauties sitting on the couch. "Skip will go, won't you, buddy?"

"Why, me and Lilly here were just getting acquainted. You go, Fred."

Mr. Fabulous-and-Fifty wrapped his around one of the voluptuous women. "Sure. Just as soon as I get Pauline a little something to drink."

"Someone should be checking him every hour at the very least, you know," Kendra said, waiting for one of the "boys" to dig deep into his sense of honor and volunteer. "Is it going to have to be me?" she prodded.

"Well, now," Skip said, rising to his feet, "that's mighty considerate of you. But"—he stuck his hand into his pants pocket—"you'll need a key to his room." He handed it over.

"Don't bother knocking," Fred advised. "Ol' Mac sleeps like the dead."

Kendra palmed the metal key, feeling the fire of her temper flare.

"Gentlemen," she said through gritted teeth, "if you'll excuse me, I'll just go make sure your friend hasn't lapsed into a coma."

She cursed them all the way down the hall, through the elevator ride, and up to Mac's door. The silence hushed her fury, leaving concern in its stead. She could hear her heart pounding as she slipped into the darkened room.

Kendra flipped on the bathroom light and used the faint illumination to make her way to the massive four-poster bed.

Mac's bulk was easily discernible beneath the thin covering of a single sheet. Lying on his side with his knees tucked up, and with one arm hugging a pillow to his chest, he was so still, so . . . rigid.

Her pulse hammered. Her muscles tensed. She approached the bed with a timidity she would have found exasperating in a first-year medical student.

"Mac?" She cleared her throat and waited for him to make a movement or a sound.

"Mac?" She touched his shoulder. His skin was cool. Too cool?

"Mac!"

He snorted, and she relaxed.

"Mac? Can you hear me?" This time, she shook him with no hesitation.

The muscles across his shoulders and in one arm flexed as he shrugged off her touch. Even in the dim light she could tell his body was as hard all over as the vast expanse of chest revealed by his movement. She'd been accurate in the description she'd given Leslie. He was gorgeous all over.

She shook him again, resisting the temptation to run her hand over the ropey muscles bunching in his arm.

"Mac!" she persisted, raising her voice. "Wake up."

His thick lashes fluttered, then lifted. His unfocused gaze settled on her for a moment before he said, "Go away." Then his eyelids closed and he sighed deeply.

"Mac, what day is it?"

Without opening his eyes he mumbled the correct answer.

"Do you know who I am?"

"The wicked witch." His voice sounded clear, his words distinct.

"Close enough." She pulled the quilt up over his shoulders and headed back to her room. She'd get

OLD DEVIL MOON • 27

a few medical supplies—and a blanket and a pillow while she was at it. She had no intention of freezing her butt off just for the privilege of playing guardian angel to a rock-headed Adonis.

He'd died and gone to hell. Waves of pain pounded through his head, sending distress signals to every part of his body. Nausea rocked his stomach. His mouth felt like a desert. He cursed every sin that had condemned him to such a place.

"Mac? Mac, open your eyes."

That voice. Its low silkiness was like a siren's song—but did sirens have devil's prongs to poke with? Something kept jabbing at his shoulder.

"Wake up, Mac. Come on. You can do it."

He tested the voice's theory. Nope. His eyes wouldn't open. Something cool and scented like a lush jungle flower pressed against his forehead. The coolness feathered over his brow before brushing his eyelids—then pulling one open so a pinpoint of light could nearly blind him.

"Geez!" He scrunched his eye closed and twisted away from the glare, sending another burst of pain shooting through his body. "Are you trying to kill me?" he roared.

A husky feminine chuckle rippled through the air. "No, Mac," the voice assured him. "I'm trying to make sure the ski didn't do more damage than we'd thought."

Renewed awareness came on the heels of the explanation, and he knew now whose voice had beckoned him.

"You can go back to sleep in a minute," Kendra told him in the sultry voice that reminded him of good whiskey—smooth and warm. "I just want to check your other pupil."

She placed her hand on his head again, and the scented coolness was like a balm. Then she rudely speared the light into his eye again.

"Hold your head still and look to the left."

"I'm in hell, right?" he said, following her instructions.

She made that sexy laughing sound and clicked off the light. "I'm sure you're feeling that way." Her hands ruffled his hair, probing his scalp in slow, thorough rotations.

His head felt the size of a watermelon. His body hurt in places he hadn't even known existed. Even his teeth ached. But there was nothing hellish about Kendra's touch. The wicked witch had become an angel of mercy.

"Are you a nurse or something?"

"Or something." The quick smile she gave him held a trace of reproach. "You should have stayed overnight in a hospital for observation."

"I don't like hospitals." He bit back a groan when he tried to straighten up.

She quit fussing over his scalp, and he immediately missed her touch. "No goose egg," she assured him. "Just a few stitches where the ski parted your scalp."

"What time is it?"

"A little after ten. You've been asleep a long time."

He could tell she wasn't pleased about that.

"What are you doing here? I thought the guys were going to check in on me."

"The guys are having too much fun down in the club room." Censure dripped from her clipped syllables, but her movements as she smoothed the blankets around him were as slow and easy as a warm Georgia breeze. "They're not the most responsible men I've ever met."

He liked the way she moved, the husky contralto of her voice. "So you got drafted?" he asked, wanting to hear her talk more than he cared about the answer.

"I was the logical choice."

"How come? We're not exactly best buddies."

She glanced up at him. Her hair fell in a short, glossy curtain that she tucked behind her ear so she could meet his gaze.

"I'm a doctor."

"Too bad."

Her hazel eyes rounded in surprise. "Excuse me?"

"I was hoping you'd decided you liked me after all."

She straightened quickly and moved away from the bed. "I'll get you some aspirin. You can't have anything stronger."

He shrugged, loosening the blankets she'd so proficiently tucked around him. "That's okay, I'm not into drugs. But I sure wouldn't mind a shot of whiskey."

Maybe it was a trick of the light, but Mac could have sworn Kendra flinched.

"You can forget about liquor," she said. "But I brought some seltzer, if you'd prefer that to water.

It might help if you feel queasy." She flipped on the light as she slipped into the bathroom, throwing a spray of white across his bed.

"Yeah, that'd be great." Although his nausea had passed, his head was pounding. "Could you make that about a dozen aspirin?"

"Two now, and we'll see when I wake you again."

"Again?" He winced, cursing himself for raising his voice and stirring the demon headache to a harder throb.

"Every other hour." She came out of the bathroom with a cellophane-wrapped glass and followed the stream of light back to his bed. Her silhouette seemed small and delicate against the bulky oak furniture dominating his room, her tread a whisper on the wooden floor.

With concise movements she unwrapped the glass and popped the top of a canned soft drink. It suddenly hit him how strange it was that she was here, in his room, taking care of him as if she really gave a damn. Doctor or no doctor, she'd made it abundantly clear that he was not her cup of tea. So why the switch?

Not that he minded. He'd been attracted to her right off the bat. But then her coolness had put him off, and this sudden change in temperature was a bit confusing. Especially when his brain was already pretty scrambled.

"Here you go. This ought to help." She offered him two white tablets and another smile.

Carefully, he eased himself higher on the bed. The blankets dropped down around his stomach, exposing his bare chest to Kendra's gaze. Should he flex a little and show her how really deserving he was of her interest? he wondered.

"Nice bruise you've got there."

He followed her gaze to a black and blue oval spreading over his left side. Great. Instead of ogling him, she was simply eyeing his bruise.

Then he glanced up and caught her wide-eyed look—and this time it wasn't directed at his bruise.

"What?" he asked, looking around for another wound.

"Nothing." Her voice sounded a little less like Scotch on the rocks and more like a whiskey chaser—a little tight, a little fast. "Are you ready for these?"

She held out her hand again, looking everywhere but at him. He reached for the tablets and felt a chill creep just below his navel. Was *that* what she'd seen? He paused to tuck the bedding back into place. Although he wasn't completely exposed, the blankets had dropped low enough to make it clear that he slept in the buff.

"I need to wet my throat first," he said, nodding toward the aspirin when she looked back down at him. She handed him the glass and he took a long swallow. "Ah. That's better." He patted his flat belly as he stared at her. Her expression was neutral. Maybe just a little too neutral?

"Amazing how the old body can crave things, isn't it?" he persisted.

Her eyes stayed trained on his face. "That's one of the things I love about medicine—the body's incredible ability to repair itself. Cravings are just one way of getting what it needs," Kendra allowed.

"You really are a doctor," he said. Yeah, she had that kind of intensity ambitious women wore like a shield. But, he decided, he'd try to overlook it for the time being.

"You didn't believe me?" she asked, her eyebrows arched.

"I guess it went in one ear and out the other."

She pursed her lips. "Maybe I should be wearing my whites and stethoscope."

A sudden image of the cold metal instrument nestled between her warm breasts brought an unexpected rush of heat to his groin.

"I—I was probably just too out of it for the information to soak in," he admitted.

"And you need to be out of it again. Take your pills, and I'll let you get back to sleep."

His fingertips brushed over her palm in search of the aspirin. So he hadn't imagined the softness stroking his scalp. And as he leaned forward, he caught a whiff of that light, exotic scent that reminded him of tropical nights under a full moon.

She waited for him to wash down the pills. Then she set his glass on the nightstand and switched off the lamp.

"Scoot back down and cover up," she instructed. "The last thing you need is a chill."

"I'm not cold, and I'm not sleepy. But you can go on back to your room." As soon as he said it he knew he didn't want her to go. He smiled wanly. "I'll be all right. I'm sure no one's ever died of a simple headache."

"You have more than a headache, Mac. You have a concussion, as well as a laceration deep enough to require stitches. You should be care-fully monitored for the next several hours." He sensed her agitation as she paced across the room toward the couch. "You shouldn't have been left alone this afternoon."

"Hey, no damage done." He suddenly felt as if she were the one in need of monitoring. She was wound up as tight as a spring. "You're certainly not responsible for what my friends did or didn't do."

She moved toward the window with a little less urgency in her stride. "True. But I knew better. They didn't."

She pulled back the curtain, letting in a stream of moonlight that flowed over her in a radiant glow. Silver beams caught in her hair, shining like tiny diamonds in the dark brown strands. She seemed even smaller, and somehow frail, in the shadowy light. He'd never been the poetic sort before, but he knew ethereal when he saw it.

"I'm not your problem," he reminded her.

"Oh, yeah?" He heard the smile in her voice. "Since when?"

Three

"Well, since we really only met today, that makes it about thirty-two years." Mac's answer was given in the same offhanded way Kendra had tossed out the question.

She turned away from the window, hoping her reaction to him was hidden in the darkness. He got to her. Little pulses of awareness thrummed along her nerves in syncopated rhythms, making her feel both foolish and tense.

"That's why I appreciate your going to so much trouble," he continued. "I'm sure you didn't come all the way from St. Louis to doctor me."

"It's okay," she said finally. "I don't have anything better to do."

"Right. You wouldn't rather be partyin' with your friends and reading a good book or anything else except waking me up every two hours."

Feeling oddly protected by the darkness, as if it

made her somehow invulnerable, she decided to be truthful.

"Actually, the book I brought isn't all that hot. And my friends aren't here to party with. So you've probably saved me from a long, boring evening."

"You're kidding." He settled himself higher in the bed and tugged at his pillows, trying to arrange them behind him. Only the slight narrowing of his eyes hinted that the movement caused him some pain. "You're here by yourself?"

"Temporarily. My friend's been delayed." Kendra moved to the bed, unable to resist the impulse to help. "Lean forward," she instructed. "I'll straighten these for you."

The pillows were warm from his body, and as she smoothed her hands over the lingering heat, her heat leaped in an unorthodox rhythm. She felt surrounded by unsullied maleness.

Hastily, she plumped the pillows into place. She felt ridiculous. She'd helped hundreds—thousands—of patients, and she'd never had any reaction other than sympathy for their discomfort. Yet here she was, carrying on like a nervous female nursing student with her first male patient.

When he leaned back into the pillows she'd arranged, he sighed blissfully. "Thanks. Do you do this for all your patients?"

She could see the devil beneath the smile he flashed at her.

"I don't consider you a patient."

"Oh, right." He nodded solemnly. "I'm a problem."

More than he could possibly imagine, Kendra thought, intrigued by the way his brown eyes sparkled and teased. They had a warmth that invited you to join in, as if nothing were so serious that a little fun couldn't make it better.

His mouth turned up at the corners, but it was his honeyed drawl that coaxed a smile from her. "How about a friendly game of cards?" He wore an irresistible cocker spaniel look possible only to males with large brown eyes and a born instinct for getting their own way.

"Fine," she said. "As long as you don't get too rowdy."

"Great. Grab a deck out of my suitcase in the closet."

"You mean now?"

"Sure. You know how to play cards, don't you?"

"Well, I . . ." She had a feeling that playing *anything* with Mac would be distinctly different from her earlier experiences—rather like playing with fire. Then again, he'd certainly kept her mind off her other problems. "I can play gin, but it's been a long time."

"Perfect. I love an easy touch."

She arched an eyebrow. "I didn't say anything about being easy."

"Even better," he said with a lazy grin. "It's no fun cheating an amateur."

"You cheat?"

"Only when it looks like I might lose."

His cocky attitude should have aggravated her, but it only made her feel like grinning back at him. "You play to win, huh?"

"Darlin', that's the only way to play."

Shaking her head, she started to go get the cards when she saw him grimace.

"Are you sure you're up to this?" She retraced her path to the side of his bed.

"Sure." He smiled sheepishly. "Just as soon as I heed Mother Nature's call."

"Let me help you," she said, reaching for the covers.

His hand shot out and caught her arm in a grip of gentle restraint. "I can manage."

He had that look—she'd seen it a thousand times—of a man who suddenly realized that various parts of his anatomy were about to be exposed to her.

She met his gaze. "I'm a doctor, Mac. I've seen it all before."

He traded her stare for stare. "Maybe so. But *it* wasn't mine."

"They're all the—"

"Don't say it."

"Well, it's true."

An arrogant gleam fired his eyes. "Not necessarily."

Laughter welled up inside her until it spilled over in a chuckle. "Okay, Mac. I'll turn my back."

He released her arm and she turned around, listening to the sheets rustle as he walked to the bathroom.

When the door clicked shut, she turned back to the bed to tidy the covers before his return. Men! she thought, caught between the urge to laugh and to roll her eyes in exasperation. Men—one of life's true enigmas. They either flaunted it when you didn't care to notice, or they hid it when it didn't matter.

Then again, would a naked MacKenzie O'Conner not matter to her?

"Kendra!"

At the summons, Kendra moved quickly to the bathroom. She rapped sharply on the door and started to open it, only to have it practically slammed in her face. Mac's fingers gripped the edge, and one eye squinted at her through the crack.

"What's wrong?" she demanded.

"Nothing that a new head wouldn't fix." He pressed his forehead against the door and took a deep breath. "If I just treat it like a bad, *bad* hangover and remember not to raise my voice above a whisper, I'll be all right."

Sympathy warred with resentment. She was all too familiar with the delicacy a dedicated drinker required. But, she reminded herself, Mac wasn't a drunk recovering from a binge. He'd been injured, and her old memories had no place in her dealings with him.

"Would you bring me a pair of jeans?" he asked quietly.

She regarded him through the crack. "I think we'd better forget the cards and get back to bed."

"*We* don't want to forget the cards. *We* don't want to go back to bed, because *we* aren't sleepy."

"But we are testy, aren't we?"

"Just get the jeans. Please," he added when she didn't budge. And then he started looking like a puppy again.

"Okay. But you have to promise you'll let me know as soon as you get tired."

"Agreed."

"And if your headache persists, you'll have to lie down and close your eyes."

"Okay."

"And if you—"

"Could you just get the jeans?"

"Certainly."

"Thank you."

"You're welcome." She gave him a long, measuring look. "And you will not cheat."

"Gin," Mac said, tossing his discard down with a flick of his wrist.

"You're cheating," Kendra accused. "No one can win honestly four times in a row."

He looked up at her through the veil of his thick lashes as he laid out his hand. "I don't have to cheat, Kendra. You stink."

"Excuse me?"

"You can't play cards worth a damn. Now pay up."

She curled her lip at him. "You have no honor. This is my last book of matches."

"Your matches or the deed to the ol' homestead, m' dear." He wiggled his brows, twirled an imaginary moustache, and leered. "Unless, of course, you wish to reconsider my proposal."

She rolled her eyes. "Just deal."

He picked up the deck and began shuffling with amazing dexterity.

"You must play a lot of cards," she observed.

"Not really." His flourishes made a lie of his words.

Fascinated, she watched him handle the deck

like a pro. Hands that looked as strong as his should be wielding a hammer, she decided, doing something that required the power visible from the tips of his fingers all the way up his muscled arms.

"What kind of work do you do?" she asked, watching his biceps and triceps flex as he played with the cards. Even his pectorals got into the act, jumping minutely when he bridged the deck and tapped it back into a smooth stack.

"I'm not a card shark, if that's what you're getting at."

"No." She lifted her gaze to his. "I was just wondering if you were in construction or something."

"Nope."

She could swear his mouth was twitching. "You're sure?"

"Trust me, darlin'. I don't do any more manual labor than I have to these days. I did enough of it when I was a kid."

"Like?"

"Bussing tables, pushing brooms. The kind of thing that keeps a kid busy and out of trouble."

"And now what? Do you play sports?"

"Only for fun."

She waited for him to elaborate, but he merely continued shuffling. He was purposely being cryptic, she decided, playing another game. She knew full well a man didn't get his kind of muscle tone from sitting behind a desk all day. So if he didn't stay in shape on the job, why didn't he just tell her he worked out? It wasn't a crime. In fact, she admired a man who took care of himself. Physical fitness was good preventive medicine.

"Look, if you don't want to tell me about your career, that's your prerogative. It was just idle curiosity."

"Okay." Mac looked down at the cards and tried not to smirk. Her curiosity was about as idle as a race car's engine on the last lap of the Indy 500. In fact, her eyes had been all over him. Good. It was about time she sat up and took notice. He'd sure hate to think he'd been pumping all that iron for nothing.

"You ever played poker?" he asked blandly, just so he could see her hazel eyes turn green.

"No."

Yep, there they went. They widened a little and then, bam, out jumped the green sparks. He'd noticed they did that whenever she was irked about something.

"Want me to teach you?" he asked innocently.

"Not particularly."

He caught the inside of his lower lip between his teeth and bit down. If she knew he was laughing at her and her snippy tone, he'd be willing to bet there'd be hell to pay. Kendra was a far cry from the easygoing type of woman he was used to.

"Ah, come on," he said with a pout to match hers. "Be a sport. I can't hack any more gin rummy."

"I think it's time you rested."

"I slept all day, I don't need any more rest. And— Oh, heck, Kendra, I'm sorry." He felt like a heel. "I bet you're worn out."

Her eyes kind of melted back into a soft, shimmering hazel. "Actually, I feel pretty good." She smiled, almost penitently. "I napped today too."

"So!" He slapped his hand on the table—then wanted to groan when an explosion of thunder echoed through his head. "Does that mean we're on?" he asked, forcing his grimace into a smile.

"I don't know, Mac. I—"

"It'll be fun. I promise." He could tell she wanted to—he could see it in the way she leaned forward in her chair. It wasn't much of a show of eagerness for most people, but he was beginning to learn that Kendra held things in pretty tight. If he'd picked up one thing from his days as a bartender, it was how to read people.

"We don't have to play for long," he coaxed. "Just till one of us starts getting tired."

"Well, I guess it would be okay."

"Great. We'll start with five-card draw. That's the easiest." He prepared to deal, but something didn't feel right. "My visor," he remembered. "I need my visor. And we'll need chips. Oh, shoot. Fred's got the chips in his room. Guess we can make do with these matches, but I've got to have my visor."

He started to get up, but a wave of dizziness hit him so hard, he felt nauseous. Kendra was at his side in an instant, coaxing him back into the chair.

"You shouldn't have stood up so quickly," she admonished. More gently she said, "I'll bet your head is killing you."

"I'll survive," he assured her. "But I've got to have my visor."

"I'll get it," she said with a sigh.

"Thanks, darlin'. You're sweet." He was surprised at how much he meant it. She really had been an angel, even when she was being prissy. In fact, he wasn't sure he didn't enjoy her prissiness almost as much as he did her gentleness.

He pointed at his duffel bag, and watched her move with her catlike grace. Damn, but she was fine. Classy. All supple lines and soft curves, even under the layer of shirt, sweater, and slacks. She'd probably sock him if she knew which way his mind was wandering.

"This can't be it," Kendra said, returning with a dilapidated looking ball cap with the top cut out. On the front was the inscription "Let The Games Begin."

"That's it," Mac assured her.

"You can't possibly wear this," she said, dropping into her chair. "It's nasty."

"I'll admit it's a bit shabby, but"—he shrugged—"I can't play poker without it."

"That's not what I mean. You can't put this on your head. You could get an infection from this . . . this . . ."

"Those are stains, Kendra. They've been there for years and the hat is clean. I throw it in the wash at least once a month."

"But it could irritate your stitches."

"I'll take my chances."

He reached over and tugged the cap out of her resisting hands, and with a level stare centered it over his head and tapped it down.

"Ooowww!" He yanked the cap off his head and launched into a colorful string of oaths she'd heard a million times before in the E.R.

"Hurt, did it?" she asked politely.

"Like a son of a— Are you laughing at me?"

She arched her brows as if truly offended. "Me? Certainly not. My job is to ease pain, not enjoy it."

His eyes narrowed.

"I did, however, tell you not to wear the hat."

"It's my lucky visor. I can't play poker without it."

"Guess we can't play then."

He slouched back in his chair and crossed his arms over his chest. "We can play."

"Gee, I don't know. Without your lucky hat, I could, quite possibly, win."

"No way!" If his face had turned to stone, his expression couldn't have been any more implacable.

"You're sure?"

"Listen up, doc. These are the rules. . . ."

An hour later she had five-card stud down pat. And she was having a blast. She looked at Mac's diminishing pile of matches and felt a real surge of satisfaction. The game was challenging, and she was getting less timid about placing her bets.

She looked at her hand and tried not to frown. A pair of threes, a pair of eights, and a ten. Nothing. Assessingly, she glanced across the table at Mac. Was he bluffing, or was he holding a royal flush?

"I'll see your two and raise you a nickel," he said, tossing in seven sticks to cover his bet.

Heart pounding, she looked at her "chips." Thirty matchsticks, maybe, and she was holding zip. What the heck. It was only a game. She counted out seven sticks, plus four more.

"Four to you," she said as calmly as possible.

He peeked over his hand and stared at her for a long, tense moment. "You're bluffing."

"Only one way to find out, pardner."

He looked at his fifteen or so sticks.

"Call."

"You rat!" She threw down her cards.

"If you can't run with the big dogs, darlin', better stay on the porch." He reached for the pile.

"Hold on there. Let's see your hand."

"Now, Kendra, you wouldn't want to upset yourself any more than you already are."

His soulful eyes weren't going to get her this time.

"Let's see, O'Conner," she insisted, trying to hold back an excited giggle.

With a twisted grin, he spread out his hand. A pair of sixes and . . . nothing! She couldn't believe it—she'd outbluffed his bluff!

Laughing aloud, she raked in the pot, flushed with victory. "You turkey! You actually thought I'd let you get away with that?"

He cocked his head and shrugged. "Hey, it was worth a try."

"You really are a cheater, you know that?"

"Me?"

She laughed at his pained expression. "Do you see any other cheaters in this room?"

"That wasn't really cheatin'. That was just testin'," he protested.

His drawl seemed to be growing thicker by the minute, and she could tell by the gingerly way he rolled his shoulders that he was tiring.

"Okay, Mac. That's it for me."

"Hey, you can't quit now. My luck's about to change."

"Sorry, we agreed. When one of us gets tired . . ."

"Just one more?"

"Not tonight." She stood, preparing to leave. But before she could take two steps, his hand closed over her shoulder. The warmth from his touch sent an incongruous shiver up her spine.

"Where you headin', doc?"

"To my room."

He angled his head toward the coach. "But your gear is here."

"Oh, right." She felt suddenly self-conscious. "I'll just get it and—"

"Why don't you stay?"

Suspicion inched over her.

"You wouldn't want me escorting you down that long, dark hall and then groping my way back here alone to fall weakly into my bed . . . or worse."

"My room is right next door. I don't need an escort."

"No, no, I'm too much of a gentleman to let you walk back there alone."

"Mac . . ."

He moved a step closer to her. "Who's going to take care of me if you leave?" He gave her a woeful look, making his earlier sad-eyed expression seem positively cheerful.

Even without the puppy-dog pout, though, he'd pushed the right button. He'd probably be fine without her, but still . . .

"Okay, I'll babysit you till morning."

He smiled. "First one up has to buy breakfast."

"Shouldn't that be the last one up?"

"No," he said, walking toward his bed. "I figure I'll sleep in."

"You're cheating again."

He grinned at her over his shoulder.

"Close your eyes, darlin'." He hooked his thumbs in the top of his jeans. "I know you're dying for a peek, but I don't feel quite at my best tonight."

She kept her eyes closed until she heard him crawl into bed. "Heaven forbid I should see you when you're not at your best."

"I like making a strong first impression."

She caught only a flash of his devilish expression before he switched off the light and the room went black.

Four

Mac tried to sleep, he really did. He kept his eyes closed, took slow, even breaths, and willed himself to relax. He blanked his mind to the kinks of discomfort from his injuries, but despite his efforts and his physical fatigue, his thoughts wouldn't settle down. Kendra Davis. *Dr.* Kendra Davis, he reminded himself. Low, smoky voice, expressive hazel eyes, slender curves, hell of a kissable mouth . . . Was she asleep? Was she wondering if he were asleep? Would they ever be sleeping together?

His eyes pried themselves open again, gradually adjusting to the dark. Shapeless shadows took on form. The couch captured his immediate attention, but he couldn't pierce the dim cavern that cradled Kendra. He listened intently, waiting for a clue that she was also lying awake in the dark. Only silence answered him.

He shifted. He scratched. He sighed.

"Are you in pain?"

With only a twinge of guilt, he welcomed the silk of her voice.

"My head hurts a little."

"I can get you some aspirin."

"It's not that bad." He rolled gingerly to his side and propped the undamaged portion of his head on his hand. "I probably wouldn't even have noticed it if your snoring hadn't kept me awake."

She let loose a gasp of outrage. "I don't snore!"

"Yes you do. Long, slow, deep snores."

From the rustling of covers and couch cushions, he figured she was lifting herself into a sitting position. "There's no way I was snoring. I haven't even been asleep yet."

He grinned in her direction. "You're sure about that?"

"Positive."

His grin broadened. So she hadn't been able to sleep either. Maybe she *had* been thinking about him. Maybe she was just as hot and bothered as he was. "I can't sleep either. I'm feeling a mite restless."

"Well, we're not playing any more cards."

"I wasn't thinking about cards."

"Oh?"

He decided he'd better not tell her what he *had* been thinking—not if he wanted to spend any more time with her.

"I was just wondering how good you really are."

"Good? At what?" Suspicion laced her tone and he couldn't blame her. Sometimes his mouth just got away from him. "If you're questioning my ability as a doctor . . ." Her voice got crisper with each word.

"No, ma'am. I can tell you're a top-rate physician. I was just thinking about tomorrow." He was scrambling. What about tomorrow? "I, uh, I was just wondering how good at . . . skiing you really are."

Her covers rustled again. "To quote your immortal word, I 'stink.' Today was my first time," she explained with a touch of defensiveness. "In fact, I'd never even been on a mountain until I got here."

"Pretty awesome, huh?"

"Awesome and glorious and intimidating as hell."

He chuckled. He couldn't see Kendra "Spitfire" Davis being intimidated by anything or anyone. "Give it another day or two. You'll own those mountains."

"Like you did today?"

"Hey, that wasn't my fault. I'm terrific on the slopes." He'd be especially terrific on Kendra's slopes—every little hill and valley of her. He shifted uncomfortably. He had to stop thinking about it. He was getting a whole new ache in the one part of his body that hadn't suffered from the accident. But Kendra's voice wouldn't let him turn his hormones off. He was certain that in bed she'd be warm and responsive and . . . "You'll be terrific too."

The lamp next to the couch flared on and Kendra squinted at him through the glare. "Are you getting a cold? Your voice sounds funny."

He grimaced, more from the raging things the

sight of her tousled hair and disarrayed clothing did to him, than from the sudden burst of light.

"Just a frog in my throat." He made clearing noises to dislodge the husky desire coating his voice. "Could you kill the light, please? I think I'm going blind, here."

The light clicked back off. "You're sure you feel okay?"

"As well as can be expected." He bent his knee to relieve the pressure building between his thighs.

"Do you really think I'll be able to learn to ski in just a few days?"

The hopeful skepticism in her voice surprised him. Where was his cool, competent Kendra? "Darlin', you'll be a natural."

"What makes you think so?"

"You've got everything it takes—style and grace and grit. And you're in good physical condition." Really fine physical condition.

"How do you know?"

"I've got eyes, darlin'. What you do for a sweater and a pair of slacks—"

"Has nothing to do with anything." Kendra flounced back on the couch, pushing away the quilt that had become unaccountably too warm. Her cheeks felt flushed. So he'd noticed her body. So . . . okay. Now they had a mutual-admiration society. No big deal. "What did you mean about grit? You can't see *that*."

"You're a doctor, aren't you?"

She rolled her eyes. "So my diploma says."

"Well, darlin', you didn't get that diploma because of your good looks." His lazy drawl picked up a pace. "In fact, I'd be willin' to bet your looks were more hindrance than help when you were battlin' with all the boys to make the grade. Unless your father was dean of the medical school or something. That could have smoothed the way a bit."

She was torn between laughing and crying at the mental image of her dad, staggering, a sloppy grin pasted on his face, as head of her medical school. "My father wasn't the dean of anything," she said with regret.

"Then you did it all on your own. And that takes grit."

Something warm and fuzzy curled up in her chest. He was right. No one had paved her way, no one had tried to make it easier for her. His simple acknowledgment of what it had taken to get her through those endless days and nights of study, work, and more study were a balm she'd been needing without even knowing it—the proverbial pat on the back. After the last few months of self-doubt and soul-searching, his compliment gave her confidence a boost.

"Grit, huh?" She sounded the word, liking the feel and taste of it. "I hadn't seen it quite that way before."

"You surely didn't see it as a stroll in the park."

"Well, no. But becoming a doctor was something I *had* to do."

"Had to? Now that's an interesting way of looking at it."

The bed groaned in the darkness and Kendra imagined Mac snuggling deeper under the covers, pulling the quilt up over his bare, muscular arms.

The sounds of rustling sheets pulled the night

closer around her, making the dark more intimate. She felt closer to Mac, closer to herself. It
was easier to give away bits of herself then.

"Why had to?" he asked. "I can see you as a little
kid, *wanting* to grow up to be a doctor someday.
But having to? Well, that's kind of strong, don't
you think?"

No stronger than the desire that had compelled
her to get out of the mire her life had become. No
stronger than the need to be something other than
"Jolly Davis's little rug rat." But even with the
sense of closeness and acceptance she got from
Mac, she couldn't bring herself to reveal that
much.

"I knew I wanted to be something other than
poor," she admitted, offering what she could. She
waited for him to comment, but his silence asked
more than any words could have. "I wanted sta-
bility," she explained. "Something I could imagine
and say 'when I get that, my life will be better.'"

"We all want something better," he murmured,
seducing her confidences with the soft lilt of his
drawl. "We all need and want to try to do better."
He sighed, as if he knew that longing. "But why
didn't you take a quicker and easier route?"

Now that sounded like the Mac she knew. It
coaxed a small laugh from her. It also coaxed an
answer.

"Well at first I thought good grades would be the
trick—you know, my life would magically change
if I could be the smartest kid in school. Then it was
being mother's little helper—keeping the house
spick-and-span while she was at work, and help-
ing her take care of my little sister. I didn't know

until Mom died that I wanted to be a doctor. But once I did realize it, it was no longer just a want, it was a need."

"Because of your mother?"

"I hated her suffering. Cancer can be such a ruthless killer. And I kept thinking, if only I knew how to cure her or at least make her feel better."

"How old were you when she died?" Mac asked gently.

"Thirteen." She felt a sudden painful longing for that lost youth, the days that had turned into year after year of struggle.

Uncomfortable with her reawakened feelings, Kendra shrugged them away. It was one thing to remember, it was another to feel the stirrings of self-pity. Her life was fine now, going just as she wanted it to . . . except for Bridgett.

"Thirteen," Mac repeated. "That's a tough age to lose a parent."

She wouldn't admit just how tough it had been. With no mother, and virtually no father, she would have been lost if she hadn't had to take care of Bridgett. "It was much more difficult for my sister," she said. "She had just turned six. I can still see the way her face looked when I tried to explain that Mom wouldn't be coming home." She sighed brokenly. "She was so afraid, and so confused."

"I imagine you were too."

She laughed mirthlessly. "Yes. But at least I understood about death. Six-year-olds can't grasp anything that final."

"Still, you were just hitting your teens."

"I don't think I ever really was a teenager. I went

from pretending to be an adult to having to be one. Nothing makes you grow up faster than trying to fill a mother's shoes."

"You must be the oldest kid in the family."

"Yes."

"Me too. It can be kind of a pain, can't it?"

Her mood lightened when she thought of the example Mac must have set for his younger siblings. Teasing would definitely have been his style, driving them nuts with his wicked tongue. How often as a child had she yearned for a loud, loving family, including an irritating older brother.

"Sometimes I wished things were different," she admitted.

"I guess you and your sister are real close."

The assumption stung. "We were. But now she thinks I'm too much of a mother hen."

"Are you?"

"I don't know," she answered truthfully. "I don't want to be. But how can I stand by and just let her drop out of college and settle for so much less than she's capable of? Bridgett is so smart, so—"

"Bridgett? That sounds suspiciously Irish to me."

Her feathers ruffled a little. "So?" she demanded.

"So, faith and begorra, me darlin', we could be kissing kin and not even know it."

"I sincerely doubt that, Mac."

"Well, that's a relief."

"What's the matter? Would it spoil your image to have a doctor on your family tree?"

"No," he answered, "but it would sure spoil a couple of fantasies."

He heard Kendra's sharp intake of breath.

"That's right, darlin'. When you and I kiss, there's not going to be anything familial about it." He knew he'd shocked her. Her absolute silence confirmed it.

"You . . . you're pretty sure of yourself, buster," she said finally.

"The only thing I'm sure of is that I'm going to kiss you. Whether you kiss me back is entirely up to you."

"Well, thank you for that."

"No problem," he assured her, wondering how green her eyes were about now.

"When did you plan on this . . . event taking place?" she demanded.

He grinned at the snippiness in her tone. "When the time is right, darlin'."

"Oh?"

"Hey, if it's bothering you that much, we can get it over with right now." He swung back the covers, just to test her reaction.

"No!" she all but shouted.

"You're right. I'm not in the mood right now," he said blithely. Like hell he wasn't. "I guess I'm ready to go to sleep now."

"You're sleepy?"

She sounded almost miffed. Good. "Yeah." He faked a yawn.

"How can you say something so . . . so . . . and then just go to sleep?"

"I'm only talking about a little kiss here, not a lifelong commitment."

The problem was, he realized with a jolt, lifelong might be just how long it would take to kiss her in all the ways he wanted. The thought made him a little nervous. Maybe he shouldn't kiss her after all. He wasn't sure he wanted to think of *anything* in those terms.

"Well, good night, then," Kendra said, giving him another hormone rush with her low, sexy voice. When she was a little rattled, her voice was even lower, even sexier. It was so low and so sexy now, he thought of ambushing her on the couch.

Better not, he decided. He clearly had some thinking to do. But he wasn't going to think about that kiss. No sirree. He was not going to think about her lips or voice anymore tonight. But those hazel-green eyes were really something. And that little freckle just above her left eyebrow . . .

"You gonna sleep all day, or what?"

Kendra decided she was hallucinating. How else could Mac sound so bright-eyed and bushy-tailed, unless maybe it was on the down side of noon. Yet every bone in her body told her it wasn't a minute before sunrise. Sighing drowsily, she ignored the dream-robber-from-hell and tried to float back into oblivion.

Footsteps thumped through her somnolent bliss.

"Come on, Kendra. Wake up. I'm hungry."

Resentfully, she opened her eyes to a clear view of Mac's vacated bed. "What does my sleeping have to do with your eating?" she asked petulantly, sweeping the room with a narrowed gaze.

"You're buyin' breakfast this mornin'," he called from the closet. "Don't you remember?"

"I remember all right." She pulled herself into a sitting position. "First one up buys."

He swung to face her, clutching a multicolored sweater in one hand and fresh white undershorts in the other.

She was hard pressed to stay as grumpy as her lack of sleep and aching muscles demanded once she got a good look at him. His rumpled hair, unshaven cheeks, half-clothed body. He looked strong and virile and oh, so kissable.

Kendra groaned. If she thought about kissing Mac one more time, she was going to lose it. Half the night had been forfeited to worrying about Mac's threatened lip-lock.

And he had probably forgotten all about it by now. He hadn't tossed and turned half the night, she knew. He probably hadn't given her a second thought after they'd said good night. He probably—

"Snap out of it, Kendra. You're not making any sense here."

"I'm not—?"

"Why would the *first* one up have to buy breakfast?"

She did snap out of it then, looking past her sleep-deprived, kiss-pondering delirium into Mac's twinkling brown eyes. "You're so full of it."

He tried to look affronted. "Me?" His sandy eyebrows arched toward his tousled hair. "I'm just tryin' to get you to own up to your responsibilities, doc. After disrupting my sleep like you did, you should feel duty-bound to feed me. Why, any reputable physician east of the Mississippi would realize it's his sworn duty to—"

"Stop!" Kendra sank back into the couch with a low groan and covered her eyes with her forearm. "It's too early for this."

"Early? Darlin', we're fast approaching the hour in which our breakfast will have to become lunch."

She peeked from under her arm. "What time is it?"

"Close to nine."

"Breakfast is served until ten-thirty."

"We need time to freshen up, Kendra." He moved from the closet to the couch and dropped his tight rear end onto the small stretch of space she wasn't occupying. "Frankly, darlin', I think it may take you a while."

Her mouth dropped open, but instead of the indignant protest she'd planned, laughter bubbled out. She could tell he was pleased with her reaction to his teasing. The twinkle in his eye flared a little brighter. "You're outrageous," she complained.

"No, ma'am. I'm a little outlandish maybe. Outstanding definitely. Out to lunch—sometimes. But outrageous?" He touched a finger to the tip of her nose. "Outrageous is the way you look good enough to eat first thing in the mornin'. Outrageous is having a mouth that just begs for long, deep kisses." He drew back and studied her heat-infused face. "Outrageous is your not knowing just how hungry you make me." The teasing glow in his eyes fanned into simmering warmth.

"Mac." His name came out in a whisper. "Mac, I . . ." Something akin to panic stirred in the pit of her stomach, but it had a heat that grew into a slow, swirling sensation.

"What, Kendra?" His mouth hovered near. "What do you want?"

"I . . . I . . ." Anxiety overwhelmed her. She wanted Mac's kiss, but she feared it even more. She was paralyzed with uncertainty, with self-conscious insecurity.

"What, Kendra? Tell me what you're thinking."

She wanted to. The light in his eyes offered understanding, offered encouragement and acceptance. But she couldn't voice her fears.

"I think you're right," she whispered, looking everywhere but at his mouth.

"Right about what, darlin'?" He stroked her cheek.

Like a nuzzling kitten, she angled her face toward his caress. Her eyes made contact with his, and she read patience in their calm glow. "I think it *will* take me quite a while to get ready."

He knew she wasn't talking about breakfast. "I can wait." He wasn't talking about breakfast either. He stroked her incredible skin one more time to appease his appetite. The silken feel of her did nothing to soothe his growing desire, but it gave him a taste, and he was willing to settle for that—for the time being. "Why don't you head on over to your room? I'll come by in about thirty minutes," he said gently.

Released from his spell, she felt pink creep up along her neck and settle in her cheeks.

"I'm really starved, Kendra. I don't think I can wait too much longer."

He was making her crazy. And he was doing it

on purpose, she knew. Were they, or were they not, talking about breakfast? She couldn't tell anymore. Well, she wasn't going to embarrass herself again by assuming he was talking about them and . . . and those appetites. "Then go on without me."

"Now you know I can't do that." He got to his feet and pulled her up after him. "You're buying."

"Oh, please, let's not get into that again."

"Okay. Let's get into the shower."

She was torn between the need to scream and the urge to laugh. "You love doing this to me, don't you?"

He cocked his head. "Doing what?"

"Playing these word games."

"Yes, ma'am, I do." He gave his answer solemnly, his expression grave. But his eyes sparkled like fireworks on the Fourth of July.

She almost let herself grin at him. "Well, you slipped up on this one, buster. You can't get into the shower."

"You mean I can't get into one with you."

She rolled her eyes. "Only *I* could end up spending my very first vacation babysitting a wounded jock who thinks he's a comedian."

"You're kidding about this being you're first vacation." He leveled a direct look at her.

"No. I've never had time before."

"And you've had to spend it doctoring me?"

"I had nothing better to do, remember?"

"Oh, man."

"It's no big deal, Mac," she assured him. "I've enjoyed spending time with you."

He searched her face. "You're sure?"

"Absolutely."

He grinned. "Want to reconsider that shower?"

"No showers for you," she said, all playfulness aside. "You've got to keep your stitches dry."

Disbelief and disgruntlement registered in his expression. "Okay," he conceded.

She didn't believe him for a minute. "I'm warning you, Mac. Don't get them wet. You could be asking for an infection."

"Okay."

"Mac, I'm serious."

He took her arm and led her to the door. "I know you're serious. You're always serious when you put on your doctor disguise. And I said okay, didn't I?"

"Yes."

"Then that's that." He opened the door for her. "I'll be by for you in thirty minutes. Be ready."

"Mac—"

"Thirty minutes." He nudged her into the hall. "And don't forget your purse."

"What are you up to?" she demanded, watching the door start to literally close in her face.

"Breakfast," he vowed softly.

She wasn't convinced. But then again, why else would he shove her out of his room? "Okay."

He closed the door, and for a moment she felt almost bereft.

"Weird," she muttered, moving down the hall to her room. "Too weird." But she wasn't certain whether she meant Mac's inscrutable behavior, or her reaction to it.

Five

Standing outside Kendra's room, Mac felt like a heel. Her very first vacation, and he had spoiled it for her. True, he hadn't asked to be knocked senseless by a runaway ski. But, still, because of him she had spent the first night of her first vacation working. Man, oh, man.

He rapped on her door, haunted by snatches of their conversation from the night before. She'd raised her younger sister, put herself through school, became a doctor at—what, twenty-five, twenty-six?—and had spent the very first night of her very first vacation taking care of him. Damn! The woman . . .

. . . looked fantastic. She'd swung the door open, and he saw the slight smile on her beautiful lips. He couldn't remember when a woman had ever looked more . . . more tempting. So untouched. She had on a navy sweater with a big white collar and a design of snowflakes and flowers. She looked like a schoolgirl, without looking childish. And the way she filled out the sweater and the red slacks she wore with it made his heart thump in a way that didn't feel childish at all.

"Ready?" he asked, almost hoping she wasn't. Then she'd have to invite him in. They'd shut the door. He'd start nibbling on her mouth and—

"Just let me get my purse."

Rats. "Great," he said. "I'm starved."

"Oh, Mac, you poor thing. You probably haven't eaten for the last twenty-four hours."

He wanted to kick himself. He had to get her to stop worrying about him and his accident. He wanted her to have nothing but fun for the rest of her vacation. He wanted to smooth that worried frown from her brow.

"I couldn't have eaten a thing last night," he assured her. "But if you hurry just a bit, I think we can make it downstairs before I start gnawing on the woodwork."

The crease of concern disappeared, and a reluctant smile parted her lips. Something inside him swelled. Pride? Protectiveness? He loved to see her smile, and he wanted to be the one to keep that smile on her face.

"Come on, darlin', unless you'd like me to start gnawing on you."

The realization that she'd very much like to feel his mouth on her skin surged through Kendra like an electrical storm, shorting out her customary reserve. It sparked an even keener awareness of him, the shape of his mouth, the curve of his jaw, the warmth of his eyes. She longed to touch his face, to let her fingers play with the thickness of his damp blond hair. She wanted to—

Damp blond hair? Her gaze was suddenly riveted on his scalp, and reality cooled her with icy fingers. "Wait here," she heard herself saying. "I'll only be a minute."

She marched across the room, slowing only when she reached the dresser, where her purse lay. She was angry. Very angry. But was that feeling even appropriate under the circumstances? She needed to put things into perspective. What business of hers was it if a fun-and-games guy wanted to play fast and loose with his health? It really wasn't her concern, she told herself firmly.

A smidgen calmer, she walked back to the door. "Ready." She pasted on a smile and ignored the way Mac's curious gaze followed her as she waltzed past him. She heard him pull the door to and felt his wary presence behind her all the way to the elevator.

Once inside the small cubicle her tension started to mount again. He was too close, too quiet. She could feel him looking at her. She refused to look back. She wanted to keep her cool. She wasn't going to make an issue of his total disregard for her professional advice. She wasn't going to say a word. Leslie would probably approve, she decided. Leslie was a great one for letting emotions cool before acting on them.

"You forgot to push the down button," she said, glancing at the control panel. That's good, she told herself. Act normal.

He reached out to touch the button with his strong, blunt-tipped finger. She was appalled at the escalation of her pulse-rate over nothing more than the sight of his hand, and she sighed impatiently.

"Is something wrong?" His question held a trace of confusion.

"Not a thing." She kept her gaze locked on the slowly closing doors.

"Then why do I get the feeling there is?"

"Guilt," she said without thinking, then quickly tried to cover her slip. "You know you're supposed to pay for breakfast."

"No, I don't think that's it."

He didn't sound too confident. Good, she thought. Let *him* stay off balance for a while. "Maybe you're reacting to your trauma. Many patients experience mood swings shortly after—"

"I'm not your patient," he reminded her. "I believe the word you used was *problem.*"

"That's true."

"I don't mean to be." His cocker-spaniel eyes almost got to her.

"Oh, sure," she argued. "That's why you took a sh—" She caught herself, then gave it up. She couldn't expect a vacation to work miracles overnight, and laying it on the line had always been her professional style. "That's why you took a shower."

"I washed," Mac conceded. He looked completely without remorse, the dimples on either side of his mouth fading in and out like a beckoning mirage. "I like being clean. But I—"

"It's not funny," she informed him, knowing those dimples were dancing because he was trying not to smile. "If you think my professional—"

The elevator lurched to a halt, and Kendra swayed from the jolt. Mac reached out a steadying hand and drew her closer to his strong, warm body. His scent cozied closer, too, and she could detect an enticing hint of cedar and spice that urged her to move even nearer. She refused its appeal and waited impatiently for the elevator doors to open. Each passing second weakened her resolve.

Open, open, open, she chanted silently to the unmoving doors.

"Did you know your eyes turn the prettiest shade of green when you get annoyed?"

Her annoyance wavered under a rush of pleasure—but he wasn't going to get around her that easily. "Don't change the subject."

His arm tightened as the elevator doors slid open. "I'm not changing anything. You're angry because I consider it my duty to bathe at least once a day, and I'm telling you you're beautiful when you're angry. Same subject, just different points of view."

She shook her head in frustration and led the way out of the car. "I give up. You don't have a serious bone in your body."

"I beg to differ." He caught her by the arm again and turned those big brown eyes on her. "There's one that—well, let's just say I take some things very seriously."

"Such as your health?"

He sighed dramatically. "So shoot me. I took a shower, but—"

"And I told you—"

"And *if* you'd let me finish, you'd know I didn't

get my stitches wet. I put the shower cap over my face instead of my hair."

"See? That's what I mean. You can't even be serious about something as important as— You what?"

"Believe me, it's not easy to breathe through plastic."

"Mac, you could have suffocated."

"But I didn't get the stitches wet."

She felt like a harpy. She'd been so full of self-righteous indignation that he'd dared to ignore her advice that she'd acted like a witch.

"I'm sorry," she murmured.

His eyes flamed. "Don't say that now."

"But I . . ." Stinging hurt closed her throat. He wasn't even going to listen her apology. "Mac," she said quickly, "I shouldn't have jumped to conclusions. I know better. I really do. Leslie keeps telling me I shouldn't shoot my mouth off—"

"Kendra—"

"—but I just can't seem to—"

"Kendra."

She opened her mouth again, only to snap it shut when he planted himself directly in front of her. A smile etched his full, firm mouth.

"You know, darlin', I've always thought an apology should be made in private, so that if there's any making up to be done, it can be done right." His gaze dropped briefly to her lips. "So don't apologize to me now unless you want me to accept your apology in the only way that would make me truly happy."

Making him happy seemed like an excellent idea. Making his eyes burn darker and hotter, making his lips move slowly and softly over hers, touching him, holding him, all seemed like excellent ideas. She swayed toward him, indifferent to the appropriateness of the place. Just one kiss. Just one. To take away all the wondering and the sidestepping and the half-fear, half-hope that had plagued her since he'd first opened his door to her.

He moved closer, close enough so the tips of her breasts brushed his chest. The contact sent frissons of excitement through her. She felt lush and feminine, as if she'd just discovered her womanhood and needed to explore its delights. His head lowered toward hers, and her breath caught in anticipation. She parted her lips, waiting for the touch of his, knowing she was tempting fate yet feeling only gratitude for the world she was about to unveil.

"Hey, Mac. The food is this-a-way. You don't want to— Oh, excuse me, ma'am."

Kendra hoped she was hallucinating. Unfortunately, she wasn't. There in the flesh stood Skip and Fred and Terry and Arthur. It was like awakening from a beautiful dream and finding a frog in your bed. She glanced unhappily at Mac, who wasn't looking any happier.

"Mornin', guys," he said. "You boys haven't been waiting for me, have you?"

"Nah. You know us better than that. I just settled up the bill and was fixing to head up to my room and check in with Susie." Terry laughed. "You know how cantankerous she can get if I don't call ever' mornin' when I'm away."

Mac smiled and looped his arm around Kendra's shoulders. "You watch what you say about my best girl there, Terry. I'm just waiting for you to slip up so I can steal her away."

Terry shot Kendra an affable glance. "Guess that blow didn't do him a lick of good. He still don't know that Susie wouldn't look twice at a skunk like him."

Kendra managed a smile, but all she wanted was to go somewhere and hide. Reality had a way of turning the most compelling impulse into an act of incredible stupidity, and playing some kind of man-hungry seductress in a public hallway was by far the most incredibly stupid, not to mention brazen, act she'd ever committed.

"Well, you guys, I'll see y'all this afternoon sometime," Mac said, easing his arm from Kendra's shoulders to her waist. A light pressure nudged her toward the restaurant. "I've got to get this woman some food before she ditches me for the next accident victim."

"You do that, boy." He nodded to Kendra. "Sure appreciate your seein' to him for us, ma'am. He ain't much to look at, but we're all pretty fond of him."

Could have fooled her, Kendra thought, remembering how they had abandoned Mac last night in order to tip a few glasses and chase a few women. Learning that one of them was married didn't raise her opinion any. "No problem," she said sweetly. With another nod, Terry headed toward the elevator.

"Now, where were we?"

The husky timbre in Mac's voice almost made her forget her embarrassment—but not quite.

"On our way to breakfast," she told him. She

couldn't bring herself to meet his gaze, but from the hefty sigh he gave, she knew he understood her temporary insanity had passed.

She was wound up tighter than a two-dollar watch. Mac watched Kendra toy with her food and had to check the impulse to reach across the table and pat her hand in sympathy. In a way, he knew how she was feeling. The tension hung over their table as heavily as the aroma of just-fried bacon. The difference was, *his* tension was due to revved-up hormones rather than the flustered embarrassment tormenting her. She hadn't been able to look him straight in the eye since they'd all but started necking in the hall.

Her gaze rose briefly from the omelet she was distributing around her plate and met his. Twin spots of color nestled in her cheeks.

"The food here is marvelous, isn't it?" she said. She poked her fork into a tiny piece of ham and eyed it as if it might bite her back.

"Better than anything I can rustle up, that's for sure."

"You cook?" This time her gaze didn't shy away when she looked at him.

Great. He'd finally hit a safe topic. "I can fend for myself. I did a lot of short-order hustling when I was in college. Nothing fancy, but it keeps me from going hungry."

That little frown he wanted to smooth away creased her forehead again. "I thought you said you'd done . . . you know . . . physical labor."

"Darlin', standin' over a hot grill trying to push

out five orders in three minutes *is* physical labor."

"Oh, well, of course." She glanced back at the ham on her fork.

So much for that topic.

He scoured his mind for something to do or say that would put things right between them again. The sputters and starts of strained conversation were beginning to grate on his nerves. The problem was, all he could think of was finishing what they'd almost started in the hallway. Her lips had been a mere breath away from his. Just one second more, one tiny little second, and he'd have tasted her. He'd have known what it felt like to hold her in his arms, to press her body closer. He would have— Hell, he would have driven himself just as crazy as his thoughts were driving him now. A public hallway was no place for getting a relationship off the ground.

Relationship? He frowned. The very word had a solidity to it. Relationships were . . . long-term, involved, complicated. Was he ready for that?

He looked at Kendra and noticed that she had completely given up on her food. She was staring out the window like a lost sailor searching for shore. He followed her gaze to the skiers dotting the mountain. That's what he and Kendra needed: some fresh air, some fun, some time to calm down and cool off.

"Kendra, why don't we get our gear together and hit the slopes?"

Her eyes widened. "Excuse me?"

Damn, but he loved the way she used those two prissy little words, sounding as if he'd said something truly outrageous and she, lady that she was, couldn't quite believe his vulgarity. It made him want to laugh, but he held himself to a smile. "I said, 'Why don't we get our gear and hit the slopes?'"

"I heard you—I just can't believe you mean it."

"Why not? Kendra, I know you're a beginner, but you don't have to worry. I'll stay right with you. We'll have a great time."

"I'm not worried." Her voice had that low, husky quality that both turned him on and also told him she was agitated about something.

"Then what's the problem?"

"You. You can't really expect to go skiing again so soon!"

He touched his stitches. "Because of this? Hey, this is nothing but a little thread."

"That closes a wound that needs time to heal."

Her eyes were like shimmering green velvet. Lord, she was something. But right now he wanted that something to calm down, to bend a little, and to let him show her a good time.

"Come on, darlin'. Put away your doctor role for a while, and let's have some good old-fashioned fun."

"There's more to life than fun, Mac. Responsible behavior is just as important as grabbing every ounce of pleasure you can. Surely even *you* can see that you have no business putting on a pair of skis for another day or two."

Only Kendra could make an insult sound like smoky sex, but the tight rush of pleasure the sound produced wasn't the only thing making him hot under the collar. His temper was stirring. "Well, excuse me for being foolish enough to think that since I can walk and talk and chew gum at the same time, I can maneuver a pair of skis over a little snow."

She raised her chin like a warrior princess ready to do battle. "I'm not talking about your skills, Mac. I'm talking about your injury. You shouldn't expose it to the elements if you can avoid it, and you can certainly avoid playing king of the mountain for a day or two."

"I could, but I'm not going to." He wadded up his napkin and dropped it on the table. "I came here for two reasons, and one of them was to enjoy something I love to do—ski."

"Well, far be it from me to stop you from going out and getting your head bashed in again. I'm only a doctor. Why should I care if you want to . . ." Her words died, and her gaze locked just over his shoulder.

He turned to find Sugar behind him.

"Well, don't let me interrupt. It was just getting good."

The tension snapped, crackled, and popped along with Sugar's gum. But then Mac darted a glance at Kendra, and his anger drained away in unison with the color in her cheeks. She looked like a schoolgirl again, only this time there was a forlorn, childlike anxiety in her eyes.

"Ah, heck, Sugar. We're just having a little difference of opinion." He winked at the waitress and gave Kendra a reassuring smile. "You know how you women are. She wants to mother me, and I want to prove I'm a big boy."

Sugar made a sound somewhere between a laugh and a bark, and her gaze swept over him with knowledgeable ease. "Honey, any woman with more than one blind eye can tell you're as big as you need to be. And this here little lady"—she pointed her pencil at Kendra—"don't look like she's in need of a seeing-eye dog to me. Now, you two need anything else, or you want to go back to your different opinions?"

"Guess we'll just take the check." He glanced at Kendra.

She nodded her agreement, then fastened her eyes on her plate.

"Okay, folks." Sugar scribbled out the bill, then slapped it facedown on the table. "You be sure and come back for lunch." Her smile was wide enough to encompass both of them. "I swear, watching you two is better than a soap opera."

With a wink and a bubble, she was gone. Mac bit down hard on the inside of his lip to keep from laughing at the feisty blonde. He did admire a woman who spoke her mind.

"I'm so embarrassed."

Kendra's quiet announcement stabbed at a tender place in his heart. He'd begun to recognize that she was a woman of both pride and insecurity, and he was certain she'd rather eat glass than draw attention to her private life. He wished he had some magic to whisk away her tension with a sweep of his hand. But all he could do was give her the truth.

"Don't worry about it, darlin'. Nobody paid any attention to us except Sugar, and she did it 'cause she's downright nosy."

She looked at him with wide, hope-filled eyes. "You think so?"

That feeling, that possessive-protective rush of emotion swamped him again. "I know so. Look around. Not a darn soul is whispering behind their hands or throwing us haughty glances." He wiggled his eyebrows, hoping she'd smile. It worked. She smiled.

"I guess you're right."

"I usually am."

She tilted her chin in that pugnacious way. "Not about the skiing."

He slumped back in his chair. Here they go again. "Okay, so maybe I'd be smarter if I sat back and played invalid today. But I'm not going to. I'm going out and enjoy the peace and the beauty and the pleasure I get from these mountains." He gave her his most enticing look. "And I want you to go with me."

She struggled. He could see it. She glanced out the window, then back at him. She sighed. She frowned. She gave him a tiny, troubled smile. "I'm sorry, Mac. But if I agree to go with you, it would be the same as giving my approval. And I just can't do that."

He sighed too. "Okay, then, I guess I'll go alone."

"I wish you wouldn't."

"I wish you would."

She almost smiled. "Truce?"

He couldn't keep himself from reaching across the table and renewing his memory of the way her skin felt under his hand. So soft, so smooth. He cupped her cheek and looked into her eyes, re-membering. She shivered a little, and he knew she was remembering too—the closeness of their lips and their bodies, the growing want that neither of them was able to hide. He wanted to kiss her so badly, he ached.

"Darlin'." He cleared his throat; aching need had lodged there. "Are we making up again?"

Kendra paced the floor of her room for over an hour before she gave up and went downstairs to the club room. It had a panoramic view of the ski trails, and maybe she could catch a glimpse of Mac.

The call of the mountains must have rung as loudly for the other guests as it had for Mac. The slopes bustled with skiers of all shapes and sizes. Sunlight sprayed through the cedars, its warm fingers caressing the snow into a glistening white and seeming to cradle each skier in smooth flight down the mountain. Kendra watched enviously, uncertain whether she was jealous of anyone and everyone who could ski with such ease, or merely begrudging them the thing they had in common with Mac—they were there and she wasn't.

Listlessly, she turned from the window, uncertain what to do. Her first impulse after separating from Mac at the restaurant had been to phone Leslie. But Leslie's service had picked up and told her that Leslie was with a patient and, unless it was an emergency, the doctor couldn't be disturbed.

Then she'd thought of calling Bridgett. But Mac's words had come back to haunt her: She'd been trying to "mother" him. That's exactly what Bridgett accused her of—over-protectiveness. She hadn't come on this vacation only for pleasure;

she'd come to give Bridgett—and herself—what Leslie called "space." With a sigh, she turned back to the window. Did Mac need space too?

The thud of booted footsteps approaching from behind her barely registered until they stopped and a small tingle raced along her shoulders.

"Okay, I admit it. You were right."

Her heart jumped. "Mac?" She turned, smiling. He looked so masculine, so rugged and handsome, with his hair slightly tousled from the wind, he almost took her breath away.

But her smile wavered as his words registered. "I was right? You mean . . ." Her gaze darted to the stitches at his temple. "Are you hurt?"

He almost snarled. "No, I'm not hurt. But the sun's too bright to ski without my goggles, and the goggles hurt my stitches." His bottom lip drooped in a little-boy pout. "I can't ski today."

She wanted to laugh, but his expression told her she'd better not. "Oh, Mac, I'm sorry."

"You are not."

He looked so rankled that she couldn't help it: She giggled.

"Now, darn it, Kendra, I knew you'd do that."

"You knew I'd laugh?"

He puffed his hair away from his forehead. "I knew you'd say 'I told you so'."

"Well, I did."

He fought a smile. She could see him battling it; his dimples gave him away. "So? You don't have to be so pleased about it. All I wanted was to have a little fun."

"Fun isn't the only thing in life."

"And neither is being right all the time."

Her good humor sank. "Is that the way I am? Do you really think I always need to be right?"

The worry in her eyes made his heart hurt. "I didn't mean it like that, Kendra. I really didn't."

"Then you don't think I'm too self-righteous?"

"No, ma'am." He leaned close, touching her cheek as he had in the restaurant.

Her breath stopped for an instant, hanging on his fingertips as they stroked her cheek. Oh, how she loved the way he touched her, the way he made her so aware of her femininity. If only he were like this all the time . . . gentle and sweet and sincere. But then, she realized, he wouldn't be Mac. He'd lose something about himself that she would miss as surely as she'd miss the sun on a rainy day: his spark, that edge that sometimes made her uneasy but that also made her laugh, gave her pleasure.

"I don't think you're self-righteous at all," he continued, letting his hand drop from her cheek to her shoulder. "You're beautiful and giving and caring. But I do think you take some things way too seriously."

She tried to smile. "And I don't think you take some things seriously enough."

He pursed his lips and nodded slowly. "You know what, darlin'? I think we may have just what the doctor ordered starin' us right in the face."

"Oh, yeah?"

"Yeah." He gave her a deep, penetrating look. Then his eyes started dancing. "I'll let you try to show me the error of my ways, so to speak, if you'll let me show you how to loosen up."

She almost laughed—until she realized that, for once, he was serious.

"You know, Kendra, having fun and being responsible aren't mutually exclusive."

"I know that. I just . . . I just . . ." She what? She didn't believe it? Couldn't let herself believe it?

The questions shook her. Had she spent so much of her life trying to prove she wasn't like her father that she'd deluded herself into thinking that all work and no fun was the only way not to turn into a wastrel?

"Okay." She made her decision quickly.

The warmth in his smile almost melted her. "You mean it?"

She stuck out her hand. He took it in his strong, warm grasp, and little prickles of excitement danced over her fingers. "I mean it."

She just hoped she wouldn't live to regret it.

Six

Regret wasn't precisely the emotion Kendra felt as she watched Mac pace the red-carpeted floor like an anxious attorney presenting his case to a hostile jury. He stopped in front of her, trying to sway her with a pleading look.

"Come on, darlin'. It'll be fun."

She shook her head, firm in her refusal, although she had to admit that, if looks alone could budge her, his would be the looks to do it. Thumbs hooked in the front pockets of his jeans, legs spread in a thoroughly male stance, he was the picture of masculine temptation.

"Okay, if you won't go for strip poker, how about spin-the-bottle?"

She bit back a smile. "No way. No strip poker, no spin-the-bottle, no post office."

He plopped down beside her on the game-room couch and looked at her hopefully. "Things-that-go-bump-in-the-night?"

She knew she'd regret it, but she couldn't help it. She bit. "What's that?"

His wicked grin told her she wasn't going to go for this plan for "fun" things to do either.

"First we turn off all the lights and close the drapes, makin' it pitch black and kind of spooky, you know?" He shifted sideways, nudging her thigh with his knee. His arm brushed her shoulder as he draped it over the back of the couch. "And then we start wandering around the room." He inched closer and lowered his voice a notch. "Nobody says a word, mind you. And it's real important that you don't giggle or do anything that would give away who you are."

She bit back a smile and nodded her understanding.

"And then, when you bump into someone, since you can't possibly know who it is, it being so dark and all, you get to start feeling around until you come across something like, oh . . . say the length of the hair, or the shape of the nose . . . until you figure it out."

She looked pointedly around the deserted room. "There's nobody here except us, Mac. I think— possibly—I might be able to tell it was you without having to do too much groping."

He sighed, absently massaging her neck with his long, sensual fingers. Ripples of pleasure fanned from his touch.

"You just don't know when to relax and go with the flow," he told her. "You just don't see—"

"I see quite well, thank you." She bowed her head, giving him better access to her tight muscles. "You don't know the difference between wholesome fun and sexual games."

He stopped kneading and looked at her as if she'd grown an extra head. "Begging your pardon, ma'am, but sex *is* wholesome fun. You, being the world-class doctor that you are, should know that better than anyone."

"I also know a con job when I hear it. Face it, Mac, you're just going to have to break down and play pool with me."

He slouched deeper into the red-and-blue plaid couch. "You don't know how to play pool."

"I don't know how to play bump-in-the-night either. You don't seem to have a problem with that."

"Well, that's different. When you're playing pool, you can't—you can't . . ." He raised his gaze to hers, and she watched his expression change from doleful to somewhere between speculative and gleeful.

She didn't like that look. "Can't what?"

"Nothing. Nothing, darlin'." He tried to look innocent, but she could see the devil dancing in his eyes.

"You're up to something."

"Now, that hurts. Have I ever tried to be sneaky about anything with you?"

"I'm not sure."

"Geez, Kendra." He looked wounded. "Didn't I come right out and tell you I wanted to get naked with you?"

She would have choked if she'd had any breath. Instant visions of taut, bare maleness intertwined with supple feminine nudity escalated her heartbeat to a hard, driving rhythm. Heat flooded her cheeks. "No! You never told me that," she insisted. But she wasn't denying him so much as she was denying her own sensual response to his question.

Mac rolled his eyes. "If I didn't want you naked, would I be trying to get you to play strip poker?"

Eventually she managed to follow his logic. "Okay," she said, once she had regained her capacity for speech. "So your intentions are . . . aboveboard. My answer stays the same." Something inside her gave a kick of rebellion, but she ignored it. "Getting naked" with Mac might not be the most irrational scenario she'd ever envisioned, but it certainly wasn't the sanest.

"Then I guess I'll have to settle for pool," he said with a dejected sigh.

Why didn't his expression match his tone? she wondered, wary. But she took his outstretched hand and tried to ignore the simmering delight that accompanied his touch.

"How much, exactly, do you know about pool?" he asked, pulling her to her feet with an ease that reminded her of just how well-toned were the muscles under his bulky ski sweater.

"Enough to be grateful there's no one around to witness my humiliation."

"Gee, thanks. I always wanted to be no one."

She squeezed his hand. "I wasn't counting you. You already know what a whiz I am at games."

His dimple winked at her. "Okay, whiz kid, the first thing you need to know about pool is how to pick the proper cue." He gestured toward a rack mounted on the wall. "Although *some* people have the mistaken idea that all sticks are the same, there is a difference, you know."

She shot him a suspicious glance before she eyed the row of identical sticks. She was sure she'd heard that argument before.

"Take this one for instance." He removed a cue from its slot. "See the tip? Worn down." He shook his head. "We can't have that."

"No, we don't want that," she agreed, noting the deficiency of that particular cue but still wondering why this process of selection seemed so pointed.

He pulled out another cue and balanced it in his hand. "Now this one . . . this one looks okay for you. Not too long, not too thick." He passed the cue to her. "What do you think?"

"Feels good," she said. It felt like a stick.

He eyed the rack for another minute and then latched on to a cue that looked identical to hers. "This one looks more like me. A shade longer, a smidge thicker."

He smiled at her in a familiar, cocky way that sent her blood rushing and her heart pounding. *Now* she remembered when they'd had this conversation.

"Okay," she conceded, not knowing whether to blush, to laugh at his arrogance, or to pet his obviously still wounded pride. "I give up. They're *not* all the same."

His smile proclaimed triumph. "See? All it takes is a little hands-on experience." And he spun away before she could do more than gasp at his innuendo.

"Now, listen up," he commanded from over his shoulder. "This is how you rack the balls."

He loaded the wooden triangular form, showed her how to chalk her cue tip, then ran through a few simple rules. After playing the first few balls to show her the general technique, he let her try her hand.

She wasn't half bad. Especially considering she was being stalked. She sensed it as surely as she felt the subtle tension each time she looked up from the table and found his gaze riveted to her. His eyes were full of a watchful intensity—an intensity that sent her pulse racing and her nerves humming.

"Want me to show you how to make that next shot?" he asked blandly when she found herself indecisive over which ball, if any, she should take a crack at.

She eyed the green felt playing surface. "There is no next shot," she concluded. "Everything's either too far from a pocket or too crooked."

"Crooked?" His brown eyes danced.

"You know what I mean. I can't make a shot unless it's straight in."

"Sure you can," he coaxed. "You just have to put a little English on the ball."

"English?" She'd heard the term before and associated it with skills well beyond the grasp of rank amateurs. "You can teach me that?"

"You bet."

The idea appealed to her. She didn't like being mediocre at anything. "Okay. Show me."

A surge of excitement sped through her when he stepped behind her, standing so close she could feel the heat from his body. He folded himself around her, leaning forward to sculpt the angle of her body over the table with a light pressure from his. His groin brushed her hips. His chest cradled her back. Fire scampered along every inch where his body touched hers.

She sucked in a sharp breath, inhaling the winter-fresh scent that clung to him like an expensive cologne. Tension sprang back in full force; coiling tighter and tighter, waiting, pulsing, throbbing.

As if sensing her disquiet, he kept his movements purposeful. He placed his hands over hers, one grasping the cue, the other cupped on the table. But it didn't matter. She was too aware of him, too consumed with the way she felt in his arms, the way his arms felt around her, so strong, so provocative, so dangerously safe.

She tried to fight her quivering awareness of his masculine power, his vibrant male strength, but she couldn't fight the sparks flying through her, illuminating the distinct differences between her body and his. She was surrounded by him, enveloped. She couldn't breathe, and she was afraid she'd suffocate in sensation.

"Now concentrate on your objective." His suede-soft voice caressed her cheek in warm puffs of air. Hot chills raced down her back.

He lifted her cue and pointed it at the target ball. His body surged against hers as he leaned farther into the table, pressing himself even more intimately against her. She felt the power in his tautly muscled form, a power previously belied by his easygoing charm. Vivid awareness of it now engulfed her.

He murmured more instructions, but she could scarcely follow them over the clamor within, her battle to stop *feeling* so much. A battle she was rapidly losing.

"Ready?" he asked softly.

She nodded, unsure what she was agreeing to under the sensual spell wrapping around her. Where was her customary caution, she wondered vaguely, her rational, analytical response to things physical? Under Mac's touch she seemed to forget reason, forget caution.

He pulled back on her cue, then guided it forward in a slow, easy lunge. His body flowed around her as fluidly as the small white ball that rushed toward its target.

In a daze she watched the opposing forces collide, one sailing out of sight into the pocket, the other rolling lazily back toward her. She waited for Mac to move again, waited for her pulse to settle. Waited . . . waited . . .

His only movement was the rhythmic stroking of his thumbs over her hands and the slight undulation of his hips, so slight she thought she might have imagined it.

"There, darlin'," he said in a voice so husky it licked over her nerves like a river of fire. "That's English."

She nodded, knowing if she spoke her voice would sound as husky and as smoky as his . . .

She twisted beneath him, wanting to face her suspicions—and she came face to face with naked desire. Mac's gaze locked with hers, confirming, challenging.

"You catch on quick, darlin'. That's one of the things I like best about you."

She was speechless. Breathless. And so caught up in the heated passion glowing in his eyes for a moment she couldn't move.

Then she tried to edge away from him, but he turned her in his arms, forcing her to reach for his shoulders for balance.

"Mac . . ." She pushed at him half-heartedly.

He locked one arm around her waist and slanted the other up her back to cradle her head. The power she'd felt earlier rippled in his arms as he held her inches away from him, controlling her, yet giving her the freedom to slip away if she chose.

But the choice was banished when she met his gaze, so dark with desire, mirroring exactly her own swirling emotions.

"Let me taste you, Kendra," he urged quietly. "Finish what you started this morning and let me taste what I can't stop thinking about."

Panic rose within her to fight the sensual hunger demolishing her inhibitions, but the panic was outgunned. One kiss, she told herself, just one. Then the war would be over and she could retreat behind the barricade of quiet competence she'd spent a lifetime building. She could regain control of her life and her emotions and go back to being sane, rational Dr. Kendra Davis, friend, sister, healer. For this one moment she would block out all resistance, all doubt that she was crossing a line she wouldn't be able to retreat behind again. She sighed her surrender.

Mac heard it. She saw the victory in his eyes. He lowered his head, his mouth so near she could feel his breath mating with hers. Her heart shuddered to a halt, and she waited to feel his lips claim hers, waited to know the touch and the taste and the texture of him—waited until his teasing hesitation drove her to close the distance between them and put her waiting to an end.

His mouth took hers with a hunger that was every dark fantasy she hadn't even known she'd had. There was nothing of quiet exploration, no playful nips, no gentle discoveries. He was black-velvet nights and tangled silken sheets. He was passion and seduction. She clung to him, unable to reason or to understand, only to feel: the hot thrust of his tongue, the hard press of his body, the excitement racing through her like bolts of white lighting until she couldn't tell the pounding of her heart from the pounding of her desire. And she wanted more.

He shifted subtly, nudging her fully beneath him. She felt treasured, captured, deliciously seduced. His pelvis brushed hers, then nestled firmly. He was hard and ready, as a slow swivel of his hips proclaimed.

"I haven't been able to think of anything but this since last night," he whispered against her neck. If this isn't what you want, too, you'd better tell me now."

Desire and confusion warred within her. She'd been clinging to him, demanding more, but could she survive more? She'd already dissolved into a pool of wanton longing.

She didn't have any answer. She did want him; every erratic beat of her heart drummed out her hunger for him. But did she want *this*? This situation? This fleeting moment of reckless abandon that could cause more chaos with her life?

"Come back to my room with me," he urged softly.

Her eyes widened, no doubt revealing all the hunger—and the fear—she fought to hide. The hunger he could appease. The fear he didn't understand.

"I'd never hurt you," he promised. "I only want to please you."

"I know." Her voice was a shaky whisper. "But it's too much. Too soon."

For an instant he pressed closer, his lips as sweet as nectar and as addictive as the hardest narcotic known to man. Then reluctantly he eased away from her, exercising the self-control she seemed incapable of.

"Too soon, huh?" He forced a smile, tamping down his frustration.

She nodded.

He could push the issue, Mac knew. Make her see she was fighting a losing battle. He knew all about this particular battle. He'd fought it himself. Wanting her, but not wanting to want so hard, so much. He also knew he'd lost the battle when the grandeur of the mountains had paled in comparison to the pleasure he found in just being with Kendra. And he'd surrendered—and come up with that cockeyed excuse about goggles in order to be with her.

Now he was finished with fighting. And that kiss had sealed his fate. He and Kendra were going to happen. It was only a matter of time. But she needed to figure that out for herself, just as he had. He wouldn't push; he wouldn't hurry. He'd bide his time.

He scowled. But time was the one thing he didn't have a whole lot of. Vacations didn't last forever.

He was tempted to toss away his good intentions, claim her mouth once more, and let them both drown in the passion of another kiss, and another, and another, until they washed up on the shore of his bed. But he caught himself. Subtlety was the order of the day, he decided. Subtle seduction and infinite patience.

"Okay, then," he said, accepting her decision— for the moment. He bit back a self-satisfied smile. "Ready for me to teach you how to make a bank shot?"

An hour later, he was inordinately proud of himself. He'd kept his hands off her—well, mostly. He'd given in to the need to touch her only once or twice. Okay, he admitted with a shrug, so maybe it was more like five or six times. But he still felt he ought to be canonized. Only a saint could resist Kendra's temptation, and he'd never been particularly saintly—until today.

He watched her round the table and pleasure rushed him head on. He liked watching her almost as much as he liked touching her. She was something. All those soft curves covering so much determination. A determination to give and heal and nurture. So many women he'd known—and men, too, for that matter—simply went after what they wanted, and to hell with anyone who got hurt.

Kendra glanced up from the pool table, and the smile she gave him wavered.

"Am I about to mess up?" she asked.

He nudged his attention to her shot. "Looks okay to me."

"Then what's wrong?"

He shook his head in confusion. "Not a thing, darlin'."

"You're tired," Kendra stated.

He pinned on a smile. "No . . . I'm just wondering if I'm ever gonna convince you to play that little poker game with me."

Her cheeks reddened prettily. "Not in this lifetime."

"That's kind of what I figured. But I haven't given up entirely on spin-the-bottle."

"What bottle is that, old buddy?" a familiar voice asked.

Mac swiveled toward the game-room door. Skip and Arthur sauntered through, accompanied by an unfamiliar woman.

"Hey, any old bottle will do," he replied to Skip. "As long as I'm not buying."

"Then name your poison," Art suggested between puffs on a glowing cigar. "This one's on Skip."

Kendra couldn't find it in her to join the good-natured chuckles. The sight of Mac's friends had dampened her good humor considerably, even before they'd mentioned liquor.

"How 'bout you, doc?" Skip asked. "We'll flag us down a hostess and set up a round for everyone."

"No, thanks." She tried to keep her tone light.

"You're sure?" Mac asked, ushering her to a high stool near the pool table. "Maybe a beer?"

She made herself smile when she told him pointedly, "I don't drink."

"At all?"

She was pleased to see only surprise in his expression instead of the disapproval she often encountered.

"I have an occasional glass of wine with dinner," she amended, settling herself onto the stool.

He shrugged. "How about some tea then? Or a soft drink?"

"A soda sounds great," she decided. "Diet."

His gaze covered her in a slow, sizzling sweep. "Is that your secret, darlin'?"

She would have been embarrassed by his blatant perusal if anyone had been paying attention, but the others were too busy sorting out their drink preference to take any notice of Mac's regard for her anatomy.

"Okay," Skip said, "that's a Scotch on the rocks for Lucy here and— Oh, this is Lucy. Lucy— Kendra. Mac, Lucy's assistant night manager here at the lodge."

"Now, what was that?" Skip picked up where he'd left off. "A diet soda and . . . What are you havin' Mac?"

"Don't worry about it. I'll get it."

"Well, that's real neighborly of you, boy."

"Not neighborly," Mac said with a laugh. "Just clearing my conscience."

Skip arched an eyebrow. "You feeling guilty about something?"

"Not yet. But I know you're gonna challenge me to a game of pool, and if I spring for the drinks now, I can take all your money later without letting it bother me."

Art slipped up behind Mac and locked an arm around his neck. "Don't think you can hustle us like you can your regulars, buddy. Don't forget who taught you everything you know."

"Are you a real hustler?" Lucy asked.

"I get lucky from time to time." Mac's easy grin as he shrugged out of Art's hold told Kendra that luck had little to do with it.

The thought made her pause. Mac *had* been pretty cryptic about what he did for a living. What if . . . ? No, no one did that for real, did they? But what about Minnesota Fats? She shook off the notion. She was jumping to all sorts of crazy conclusions again.

"You don't mind if I take a minute or two to fleece these guys, do you, darlin'?" Mac asked.

She shook her head, trying not to show how uncomfortable she was. The game room had taken on a different flavor the minute Mac's friends had arrived. All she wanted was to get away from them and away from her thoughts. She longed for the quiet camaraderie she and Mac had been enjoying. But Mac *had* come to the lodge with his friends, and she'd had quite a bit of his undivided attention.

"Go ahead," she said, forcing a smile. "I've never watched a hustler before."

He cocked his head, giving her a sizzling private look. "Darlin', you've not only watched my best hustle, you've beaten it."

"Well, hell. Maybe we should play you, doc," Skip suggested, missing the nuance.

"Not a chance," Mac answered for her. "She's saving it for a rematch with me." He gave her a wink before turning to the door. "Keep an eye on these two while I'm gone. If there's a way to cheat, they'll find it."

By the time Mac returned with the drinks, Skip and Arthur had already played a few warm-up shots, and Lucy had taken root on the stool next to Kendra's.

"And then I ended up in Colorado," Lucy was saying. "Who'd have thought a native Floridian would end up in these mountains, for pete's sake. But I like it here." She took a sip of her Scotch and turned to Kendra. "There's always something to keep me occupied."

Kendra willed her stomach to settle down when Lucy's Scotch laced breath washed over her. She glanced toward Mac, remembering just how busy he'd kept her since his accident, but even his dimpled smile couldn't dissipate her uneasiness. There were too many memories tied in with the smell of hard liquor for so few new ones, no matter how pleasant, to push them aside.

"Come on, Mac," Skip called from the pool table. "I've decided to be the first to whip you."

"Dream on," Mac shot back, already turning toward the table.

"I just love watching a good game of pool, don't you?" Lucy asked, lighting the cigarette she'd wedged between her lips.

Kendra sipped her soft drink to avoid answering. Until she'd played with Mac, she'd never watched an entire pool game in her life. She'd never wanted to stick around pool halls or bars that long.

"I'm putting my money on you, boy," Art said, slapping Mac's back before edging past him to join Kendra and Lucy. "Don't let me down."

"Not a chance," Mac promised. He picked up his cue and chalked it.

Art took a stance next to Kendra. The bluish haze of his cigar smoke clouded the air along with Lucy's cigarette. The mug of beer he waved toward the table when Mac made a powerful break sloshed in unison with Kendra's stomach. Tiny beads of perspiration broke out on her forehead.

"He *is* good, isn't he?" Lucy murmured.

Skip wandered over from the table and gave Lucy a leering smile. "He may *look* good," he said with a wink. "But you shouldn't judge a book only by its cover."

Kendra's stomach dropped to the floor, and nausea rose up to fill the vacancy. The unmistakable odor of bourbon laced the air with every word out of Skip's mouth. Bourbon. The smell her father had always worn when he come home from a binge. The stench that had filled the neighborhood bar when she'd had to hunt her father down and bring him home to her ailing mother or her scared little sister.

She slipped off the stool, forcing herself to take

short, shallow breaths so she wouldn't inhale too deeply of the liquor and the smoke.

"Excuse me," she murmured carefully. "I think I'll go up to my room."

Mac glanced up from the table, and with one brief look he dropped his cue. "Are you okay, darlin'?" he asked, moving quickly toward her. "You look pale."

"I'm fine," she lied. "I just need to go to my room for a minute."

"I'll go with you. You really do look—"

"No!" She knew she'd sounded too adamant when she saw the surprised hurt in his eyes. She gave him a weak smile and lowered her voice. "Stay and finish your game. I'll be fine."

Her stomach took a final heave, and she knew she had to start moving. Now.

Seven

If she didn't come out of there soon, Mac decided, he was going to have to go in and get her. That's all there was to it.

"Kendra?" he called, giving the door another sharp rap. "Please, darlin'. Just let me see that you're all right." The silence greeting him made his heart pump faster, and it was already racing at breakneck speed. "Kendra? I want to see you. Now."

To his relief, the door swung open.

"Look, bub." A woman in a lodge uniform glared up at him. "She's sick. You want to hold her head over the toilet, that's fine with me. But wait till I finish my business."

The door swished shut in his face. He bounced it back open with a slap of his palm.

"Hey, you can't—"

"Well, I am." He edged past the employee into the powder area. "Where is she?"

The dour-faced woman angled her head toward another door. He took a hesitant step.

"Well, hell, macho man. No need to get weak-kneed now. Ain't nobody in there but her."

He sighed his thanks, nudged the second door open, and made a quick surveillance. Kendra was leaning over the sink, splashing water on her color-less cheeks. His stomach knotted. She looked so frail.

He took a deep breath. "Do you need some help?" he asked, venturing into the forbidden territory.

Kendra looked at him with swollen, red-rimmed eyes. His heart rolled over.

"I'm okay now," she said.

Her voice sounded scratchy, and heaven help him, sexy. She could look like the devil, sound like sandpaper, and he still found her sexy.

He went to her and gently placed his hand on her forehead. "You don't feel like you have a temperature or anything."

She shook her head, lifting her wobbly gaze to his. "I really am feeling better. But you don't look so hot."

He'd die before he'd let her know how upset he was at seeing her this way. "What do you expect?" he improvised. "I'm standing in the middle of the ladies' room. So what do you think? Could you maybe finish being sick somewhere else?"

"I think I'm all finished."

He breathed a sigh of relief, but he noted that her face was still pale and her hand trembled when she lifted it to tuck some hair behind her ear.

OLD DEVIL MOON • 101

"Come on, darlin'." He wrapped an arm around her shoulders, prepared to carry her if necessary. "I'll help you to your room."

"Don't be silly." She tried to smile. "Go back to your game. I'll be fine now."

"Like hell. You're sick. Maybe you have food poisoning or something. I'm not about to leave you until we find out what's wrong." He led her out both doors, walking slowly.

"It's not food poisoning," she said quietly.

The certainty in her voice made him a bit calmer. She *knew* what was wrong. Of course she did. She was a doctor. Doctors knew all about being sick, didn't they?

"Well it's not the flu. You'd have a fever if it was the flu, wouldn't you?"

"Yes, I would. And no, it's not."

He gave another thankful sigh as they entered a waiting elevator. No flu. No food poisoning. It probably wasn't anything serious. Just a little tummy problem, or—"Are you . . . pregnant?"

"No."

She sounded firm, and he was utterly confused.

"Then what is it, darlin'?" he asked as they walked into her room. He urged her to stretch out on the bed, pulled off her shoes, then tucked the bedspread around her. He sat next to her, taking one of her hands in his. "How can I help you if I don't know what it is?"

To his horror, her eyes teared up.

"There's nothing you can do to help, Mac. It's just . . ." She tried to laugh, but it only seemed to make the tears in her big green eyes well thicker and faster, until they rolled down her cheeks. "Oh, it's so stupid. And so hard to talk about."

When he felt a faint shudder quiver through her, he stretched out beside her, nestling her head into the curve of his neck and snuggling her quilt-wrapped body closer to his. He stroked her back through the covers, willing the tremors away.

"Tell me, Kendra. There's nothin' you can't tell me." He combed his fingers gently through her soft, silky hair, wanting to help her more than he'd wanted anything in a long time.

She gave a long, shaky sigh. "It was the smell."

He stopped stroking, totally confused. "What smell?"

She angled her head to look into his eyes. "The smoke. The liquor."

A knot of apprehension ballooned in his stomach, but he waited silently for her to explain.

"It usually doesn't bother me so much anymore," she continued. "At least, not like it did today." Her eyebrows knitted again. "Maybe it was the pool room." She took a deep breath. "And the bourbon," she admitted.

She searched his gaze, imploring him for understanding. And as soon as he understood, he'd give it to her. If he had to go out and wrestle all the demons in hell for her, he'd get whatever it was she needed and lay it at her feet.

"My dad always smelled of bourbon," she said softly, almost fearfully. "He was . . . he was an alcoholic."

Mac closed his eyes against a wave of incredulity. Oh, Lord. How was he supposed to tell the woman he was crazy about, a woman who obviously had deep wounds due to her father's alcoholism, that he'd virtually grown up in bars? His first after-school job had been bussing tables at the neighborhood pub. And then, after a stint of short-order cooking, he'd graduated to bartender. He'd served drinks to men just like Kendra's father.

"Did your dad ever . . . hurt you?" he asked, dreading the worst.

She shook her head. "He wasn't a mean drunk. Or an ugly drunk. He was just a drunk."

"And the smell of bourbon made you think about him? And that made you sick?" He wanted to shove his fist under the faceless man's nose and force him to see what his disease had done to his daughter. And he wanted to stop feeling this ridiculous sense of guilt.

Kendra pulled away from him, raising her chin in that way of hers. "No, that's not what I mean. I mean . . . I told you, it's not usually like this." She rubbed her temple. "You have to understand. I loved my dad. There were times when he was so wonderful. Sober or drunk, he was a sweet man, funny and charming. A little like you," she said with a small smile.

Oh, great, he thought, feeling his discomfort tighten. She was comparing him to an alcoholic.

"He could make me laugh," she said, her eyes lightening. "Even when Mama was having a really bad day, he could always make us laugh." Her eyes darkened again. "Unfortunately, he made everyone else laugh too." She shook her head. "Leslie says that's why I'm so driven to make something of myself and to see to it that Bridgett lives up to her potential. I hate being laughed at."

He took her hand and looked into her questioning eyes. "I want you to understand something." He held her gaze, willing her to hear his sincerity. "Just because you make me laugh a lot, that doesn't mean I'm ever laughin' *at* you. I just like the things you do and the way you do them. Got that?"

She held his gaze for a long moment, then nodded.

He sighed with relief and tugged on her hand. She came back into his arms without resistance. "You know, darlin', nobody else would have laughed at you either, if they'd only realized your dad was sick."

"Yes, he was sick. But I didn't know that back then. All I knew was that he couldn't hold down a job, he couldn't keep a decent roof over our heads, and he broke just about every promise he ever made."

"The day my mother died, he was out on a binge. There wasn't any money for hospitals, so Mama was home. That day, I don't know, I guess I just had a feeling . . . so I stayed home from school." She shivered. "I had to go find him. He was so drunk I couldn't get him to leave the bar, even though I told him . . . I *told* him . . ."

Mac wanted to do something. Say something. But he knew she needed to talk, and she needed for him to listen. He listened, even though each word tightened his nerves to wire-thin cords.

"All he cared about was one more bourbon," she continued. "His wife was dying, and he wouldn't leave that crummy bar and his booze to come home and help her." She sighed. "To this day I can't go near a bar without thinking about it. I guess that's why I overreacted today. It was the smell, the same sounds."

He held himself very still. What could he do? Say, "Oh, by the way, Kendra, that bar sounds just like the first place I ever owned. But don't worry, I've graduated to high-class pubs."

He tried to push the worry aside. His pubs had nothing to do with Kendra's father.

"I tried to hide Dad's problem from Bridgett," Kendra said. "I've spent half my childhood and all of my adult life up until the day he died trying to shield her from the jokes about poor old Jolly Davis." She laughed mockingly. "And now she resents it. She says I'm overprotective. That I can't live her life for her."

"You can't," he told her softly. "You have to let her find her own way."

"That's what Leslie says."

He arched an eyebrow. "Who is this Leslie you keep talking about?"

"My best friend. And a top-notch psychiatrist."

"Well, she's a smart cookie. Take it from me— you can't make someone into something they don't want to be, no matter how hard you try."

She stacked both hands on his chest and propped her chin on them, bringing her eyes level with his. Her eyes had a soft, slumberous look to them, and he became doubly conscious that they were in a bedroom on a bed. Her breasts innocently rested against his ribs, and he knew she didn't have a clue what she was doing to him. His heart kicked into a harder rhythm. He shut his eyes. Damn his perverted hide.

"You sound like you've been down that road," Kendra said, trying to hide a yawn. "Did someone try to convince you there was more to life than hustling pool?"

He chuckled. "My dad tried to convince me to become the 'and Son' at O'Conner's Auto Repair. Only problem was, I didn't want to be a mechanic." He opened one eye and squinted at her. "And I'm not a pool hustler." *I'm a bar owner.* He cursed his wayward thoughts and forced a smile. "I'm just good."

"Better than you are at being a mechanic?"

"I'm good at that too. But my brother Mike's better. He's the 'and Son.'"

She snuggled her cheek against his chest. "So, what do you do?"

His heart lurched. "Why don't you just rest now, darlin'," We'll talk later."

"When?"

"After our nap."

"We're going to sleep?"

He nodded.

She yawned again. "We are kind of tired, aren't we?"

"We didn't get all our beauty sleep last night."

"Last night seems a million years away," she said sleepily.

"It is, darlin', it is." He stroked her soft hair while her breathing deepened and regulated. He just hoped their next night together wouldn't be another million years away.

• • •

"Looks like you folks will have to wait here while I get some help." The driver of the dead-as-a-doornail station wagon twisted around to face Kendra and Mac from over the front seat. "It's the choke. She won't start again without a jump."

Kendra sighed. Why didn't it surprise her that the lodge's only means of transportation worked about as well as the heating system?

"How long will it take?" Mac asked, temporarily robbing her of his warmth when he leaned toward the driver.

The driver scrunched his forehead. "Oh, not much more than thirty, forty-five minutes. Sam's Garage is already closed. Might take me a while to track him down."

Mac reached for the door handle. "That's okay. We'll walk."

Kendra popped forward in the seat. "We'll what?"

"Walk," Mac replied calmly.

"To town?" She glanced past her crepe de chine evening pants to her three-inch heels.

"It's only a little farther." He climbed out of the car and extended his hand to her. "We can be at the restaurant in no time."

She took his hand but didn't climb out after him. "I can't walk down that hill in these heels."

His gaze moved down to her shoes, then bounced to the steep, snow-dusted walkways. One side of his mouth kicked up in a pensive scowl. "It could get kind of tricky, huh?"

"Suicidal comes closer."

He nodded. "Well, there's only one thing to do."

He tugged on her hand, pulling her to the edge of the seat. "Stand in the door frame," he instructed, turning his back toward her. "Then climb on."

"Do what?"

He swiveled his head to grin at her over his shoulder. "When's the last time you had a piggyback ride?"

"You're not serious." She laughed with surprise and disbelief. "You're going to *carry* me to town?"

His grin widened, flashing warm and wicked in the silver moonlight. "Sure. If you feel too guilty about it, you can carry me back up."

"Oh, right." But, feeling as giddy as a three-year-old, she did as he said. Two days ago, she wouldn't have dreamed of doing something so wild. But then, two days ago, she hadn't known Mac. It was odd, but ever since she'd awakened from her nap, still cradled in his arms, she'd felt as if a weight had been lifted from her—a weight she hadn't realized she'd been carrying until he'd taken it from her with his unquestioning acceptance of who she was and how she'd come to be that way.

She loosely wrapped her arms around his neck, and he gripped her knees in the bends of his arms as he lifted her from the car.

"This is crazy!" she said with another laugh. "And my feet are still going to freeze."

Snow crunched under Mac's feet as he stepped away from the car. "That's what you get for wearin' sissy shoes."

"They're not sissy," she said, raising a foot to

admire the stylish pumps. "They're extremely fashionable."

He hefted her higher on his back. "For a city slicker maybe. But these are the mountains. How did you think you'd get anywhere in a little bit of nothing like those shoes?"

"The lodge is fully self-contained," she reminded him, quoting the infamous sales brochure. "I didn't think I'd have occasion to be trekking into town."

"Well, hang on tight, darlin', 'cause you're about to trek."

He stepped up onto the walkway and skidded on the dusting of snow. Kendra screeched, but Mac only chuckled as he veered sideways, then smoothly regained his balance.

"You folks are gonna break your fool necks!" the driver called from the car.

"She's gonna choke me to death first," Mac answered, already headed down the walk.

Kendra immediately loosened her death grip.

"I can see you're about as experienced at piggy-backing as you are at pool." He shook his head. "Now, I'm gonna hoist you a little higher and then I want you to loop those arms around me, but only for balance. You hang on with your legs. Okay?"

He moved her up his back, and her legs settled at his waist, pitching her forward enough that her cheek brushed his. His skin was smooth from a recent shave and the scent of his cologne tantalized her with hints of musk and spice.

"There," he said, taking off in an even stride. "That's better."

"And warmer." Her breasts were snuggled

against his back, and even through the bulk of their coats she could feel his body heat.

From the corner of her eye she could see his strong profile—the straight cut of his nose, the full curve of his mouth. The memory of the way that mouth had felt on hers, hot with passion and demanding her own passion in return, touched her with fingers of desire. Her blood warmed, pooling in a sweet, low ache that made her restless with wanting. She snuggled her face into his neck, tempted to kiss the pulse point beneath the curve of his jaw.

"Just hang on, darlin'." He nodded toward the town. "We'll be there in a minute."

She followed his gaze to the scene stretching out below them. It must have been a picture-book Swiss village. Old fashioned streetlamps dotted the wooden walkway into town and lighted the quaint storefronts. A full, winter moon lent a silvery glow. Only an occasional neon sign detracted from the rustic simplicity.

A few cars were parked in front of shops, and people strolled along, their laughter drifting upward.

"I didn't realize it would be like this," she said softly. "It's so pretty. And so busy."

"Denning has a population of about fifteen hundred permanent residents, but the lodges and resorts keep the head count at close to three or four times that during both the winter and summer months."

She shot him a surprised glance. "You sound like a spokesman for the Chamber of Commerce."

He shrugged. "I like to know about the places I visit."

He reached a flight of steps. "Hang on darlin', this might be tricky."

"Oh, put me down. You can't—"

"Are you doubting my manly capabilities?" The gleam in his eye was positively wicked.

"Oh, no," she promised. "Never."

"Your lips are twitching."

She pulled her mouth into a line.

"Too late," he warned her.

She had just enough time to tighten her hold before he started jogging down the steps, bouncing an excited giggle out of her with each quick footfall. She closed her eyes and hung on for dear life, relishing each reckless moment of their downhill flight.

They reached the bottom without mishap.

"That'll teach you to doubt me," he announced.

"But I didn't," she said with a smile. And she realized she hadn't, not for a moment. She felt safe with him. Safe and more secure than she could ever remember feeling.

"There's the restaurant." Mac nodded toward a side street.

A sign in old English script hung over double smoked-glass doors.

"Bear's Den?" Kendra asked.

"That's it, thank goodness."

"Why, Mac. Are you tired?" She laced her voice with mock incredulity.

"Me? Hey, I could jog up and down that mountain with a grizzly bear strapped to my back and never miss a step." He hoisted her a little higher. "Just how much *do* you weigh, anyhow?"

She retaliated without thinking, playfully sinking her teeth into his earlobe.

A shiver ran through his shoulders. "Do that again, darlin, and we'll see how fast I can jog back up that hill."

Her surprised gasp almost broke her hold. "Oh . . . you . . ."

He stepped up to the curb in front of the restaurant. "Want to go in, or try for the lodge?"

"Are you kidding? I'm starved." She tried to ignore the fact that her own hunger suddenly had little to do with food. The warmth of Mac's body between her legs, the feel of her breasts pressing against his back, the strength of his arms locked around her thighs, were powerful appetizers for a main course that made her nearly light-headed with longing.

He stooped down to deposit her on the sidewalk, and she slid down his back. The sensual friction made her gasp.

Drawing the wrong conclusion Mac flinched, immediately worried. "Oh, darlin', I'm sorry." He shook his head. "Looks like I should have done more thinking when I planned this surprise outing."

Kendra attempted to smile, wishing she could let him off the hook, but unable to tell him the truth. "You couldn't have known the car would break down. Besides," she said, "I'm okay now."

He took her arm, still cursing himself. "Let's get inside before you get frost-bite."

He ushered her through the smoked-glass

doors. The Bear's Den was busier than he'd expected it to be. It was well past the dinner hour, yet the reception area had several parties waiting to be seated. He smiled happily, glad he'd phoned ahead. He stepped up to the hostess's podium.

"How many in your party, sir?" the attractive redhead asked with a welcoming smile.

"Two. And I have a reservation," he told her. "Under O'Conner."

The hostess ran her gaze down the reservation book. "I'm sorry, sir. I don't find your name."

He stared at her in disbelief. "O'Conner," he repeated, thinking she must have misunderstood. "MacKenzie O'Conner. Dinner for two. At eight."

She ran her finger down the page. "Oh, here it is." She flashed him an apologetic smile. "Under MacKenzie. I guess the party you spoke with must have misunderstood."

Mac pinned on a smile and tried not to show his irritation. "These things happen."

"Not often, sir. I assure you."

He was glad of that.

"This is nice," Kendra said, after they'd been seated in one of the quieter sections of the restaurant.

"Cozy," he agreed, pleased with her reaction. He'd decided showing was better than telling in this instance.

He watched her take in the rough-hewn cedar beams, the bric-a-brac reminiscent of old England, and the waiters and waitresses in period costume.

"It's just like a pub," she commented. "It sure isn't like any of the bars my dad ever frequented."

His spirits hovered between relief and uncertainty. "You do like it, don't you?"

She nodded. "Of course."

"Good." He breathed a sigh of relief. "What would you think if I told you I owned it?"

She looked at him blankly. "Owned what?"

"This pub. It's mine." He smiled, waiting for his news to sink in. He could tell the moment it did. Her eyes widened, and then she blinked. The corners of her mouth lifted prettily.

"Of course it is," she said sweetly. "That's why they got your name wrong on the reservation list."

He laughed self-consciously. "That was just a little mix-up. It could have happened to anyone."

She laughed too. "To the owner?"

He started to feel a little miffed. "You don't believe me, do you," he said incredulously.

"Now, why would you think that?" Her eyes crinkled with humor. "Just because you live in Georgia and this restaurant is in Colorado? Or just because you've made it some kind of game not to tell me what you do for a living? Or just because the people who supposedly work for you don't know you from Adam? Why should I doubt you?"

"You shouldn't," he stated firmly.

He could tell by the grave way she nodded that she didn't believe him for a minute.

Eight

"This is wonderful," Kendra said, spearing a tiny bite of Hawaiian-baked chicken with her fork. She held it toward him. "Want a taste?"

"I know how good it is. That's why I had it put on the menu."

Her hazel eyes sparkled. "Oh, of course."

She was humoring him, he knew. Just as she had been for the last thirty minutes. Didn't she want to believe he was successful enough to own Bear's Den? "Dammit, Kendra. I *own* this place."

She put down her fork, obviously surprised at his outburst. Her forehead wrinkled in a frown.

"Then why didn't you tell me the first time I asked you what you did?"

He shrugged. "It seemed like a good idea at the time."

"You were teasing me," she reminded him. "Again."

"So I like to tease. Is that a crime?"

She smiled and touched his hand. His pulse kicked into higher gear. Damn, but she got to him.

"It would be a crime if you didn't tease," she said softly. "Your eyes were made for mischief. And your dimples." Her smile widened. "And that cocky grin of yours."

He was wearing that grin now, he knew, as he laced his fingers through hers. The texture of her skin knocked him out, it was so soft and smooth. Other parts of her would be even softer. Her breasts would feel like warm silk, with velvet tips the same pale shade of coral as her mouth. Her mouth . . . Oh, Lord. His pulse revved higher. He could still taste her sweetness, still feel the way her lips had parted under his, and the way her tongue had mated with his—with the same hunger he'd brought to her.

He sucked in a sharp breath of desire. Hell, maybe it was no wonder she didn't take him seriously. Every time he looked at her he turned into a space cadet, blasting off into sex-starved orbit. His hormones running rampant had to stop. Or slow down—at least until Kendra was ready to catch up with him. Otherwise he was going to drown in unrequited longing.

Geez. Unrequited longing? When had he ever used those words? He'd become a new man around Kendra, a man who could think well beyond one-night stands to countless nights.

"You like my grin, huh?" He knew he was going to fluster her, but he couldn't help it. She flustered him.

To his surprise, she smiled and said, "And your eyes."

Kendra couldn't believe she was being so forward again, but she seemed to be a different person with Mac. She went into erotic recall every time she looked at his mouth. He brought out a sensual woman in her she hadn't known she was hiding. A woman who wanted . . . Her gaze wandered to her plate.

"Have you changed your mind?"

Mac was wearing his puppy-dog pout. "Changed my mind?" she asked.

"About my eyes and my smile," he said.

"Of course not."

"You're frowning." He toyed with her fingers. "How come?"

She sighed and shook her head, irritated with herself. She didn't want to spoil the evening by thinking about her problems. "My mind strayed," she admitted.

"Bridgett?" he asked.

She laughed with surprise. "No. In fact, I haven't worried about her since . . ."

"Since I first dazzled you with my manly charms?" He grinned his cocky grin.

"Oh, at least since then."

"Then let me dazzle you some more." He kept his grin in place, but his laughing eyes became softly serious. "Tell Dr. O'Conner all about it."

"It's nothing, Mac. Just . . . job related."

He glanced heavenward. "Then you *have* to tell me. I don't want to go through any more of this job stuff."

"I'm not the one who's been making a big secret—"

"No more secrets—I've confessed. Now you have to."

She still wasn't sure she believed him about the Bear's Den, but she did believe he wanted to know what was troubling her.

"I'm undecided."

He regarded her thoughtfully. "And . . . ?"

"That's it. Undecided."

"Right. You, who's known what you wanted to be since you were thirteen years old, are undecided about something."

She smiled uncomfortably. "I know. It's not like me. But ever since Bridgett told me she was dropping out of college and moving out on her own, I can't seem to get my priorities back into order."

"You've lost me. You said this wasn't about Bridgett."

"It's not. Not really." She shook her head, feeling the same confusion she knew she was causing in him. "It's just that I've been offered an opportunity to go into private practice, and I . . . I'm stalling. I can't seem to make a decision."

"Maybe you don't want to go into private practice."

"That's just it. I should want it," she told him. "I could give up my residency and have normal hours, a normal life. But now, I don't know."

"Then maybe you don't want to be with this particular practice."

Everything he was saying was logical, following the same patterns she'd followed herself. But the logic hadn't worked then, and it wasn't working now. "I just don't know. Everything's changing all at once—my plans for Bridgett, my career opportunities. I feel like everything's snowballing, and I've got no control over how fast it rolls." Frustration with herself built into tension. She squeezed his hand, finding release in his resilient strength.

He squeezed back, drawing her gaze to their interlocked fingers. She loved his hands—their shape, their size, the way they made her own look so small and feminine.

"Maybe you're scared," he said with another soft squeeze.

She jerked her gaze back to his. "Of what?"

He shrugged. "Change. Failure. Sometimes it's hard to take the plunge when you're not sure how deep the water is."

She felt a stinging in her eyes and tried to laugh it away. She couldn't be getting maudlin over a simple statement. But she knew, even as she tried to deny it, that his insight had touched her. She didn't want to be a coward. And, deep down, she was terrified she was.

She decided to sidestep her insecurity with a teasing smile. "I bet you plunge without even looking."

"Oh, I look." His eyes made a slow perusal of her. "I always look."

Just the touch of his gaze left an invisible trail of heat simmering along its path.

"And I want to plunge right now. With you."

The rhythm of her heart surged so strongly, she wondered if it had ever really beaten before.

"But some things take time." He walked his gaze over her again. "Even when it's meant to be."

"Your confidence is amazing," she said, not

quite able to keep a touch of huskiness from her tone.

His dimples peeked from each side of his tempting mouth. "It's not confidence, darlin'. It's more like hope."

"Pretty darn certain hope, if you ask me."

"Hey, if I didn't have it, I'd probably be lying under some car right now instead of sittin' here with you. Or I'd think that owning a pub or two was the best I could do. But I think there's more. And I'm willin' to take chances to get it."

"Get what?" she asked, intrigued by the intensity of his tone.

"Somethin' different. Somethin' a little more uptown."

"Excuse me?"

He smiled, and the excitement glowing in his rich cocoa eyes added animation to his face.

"I want it to be classy," he said. "Kind of in between Antoine's and Sardi's. Lots of atmosphere. Great food by a really great chef. High class, high dollar. That kind of thing."

"Sounds exciting," she agreed. "But wouldn't it be risky?"

He leaned forward in his chair. "Anything worth doing has a certain amount of risk. But in the right location, with the right promotion, it'll work. I know it will."

His enthusiasm was contagious. "Have you found a suitable location?"

He shrugged. "Not yet. At least, not one we can all agree on."

"We?"

"Me and the guys."

Doubt pricked her. "The guys?"

"My investors. Fred, Terry, Art, and—"

"Skip," she concluded.

She had the picture now. Mac had big dreams and not enough capital, and he was counting on his so-called friends to pitch in.

She shook her head in disappointment for Mac. "I hate to dampen your spirits, but do you really think you can depend on those guys to come through for you?"

"Now, Kendra, I know you haven't exactly gotten off on the right foot with them, but they're all good ol' boys."

"And completely irresponsible. Look at how they abandoned you yesterday. And then today . . ." She shuddered.

"They were entertaining Lucy," he insisted.

She rolled her eyes. "To what ends? A little hanky-pan—"

"Getting information on the lodge."

That stopped her. "What?"

He raised his right hand. "It's true. We came up here to see if it would be profitable to try to turn this lodge around. In case you hadn't noticed, it's a little run down. Ol' Fred has always had a yen for a place in the mountains, so when I told him about—"

"What about *this* place?"

Mack cocked his head.

"You said they're your investors. Does that mean ol' Fred owns a piece of the Bear's Den?"

"Well, no, actually. He'd just taken a setback on some oil deals, and his reserves were pretty well tied up."

"And the others? We can't forget Art and Terry and Skip. Were they also low on reserves?"

Mac slumped back in his chair. "Sort of," he admitted reluctantly. "Skip was in on the same oil deals as Fred."

"So Art and Terry own a third of Bear's Den along with you?"

"Not quite."

She arched an eyebrow. "Oh?"

He sighed. "A little less than a third."

"Oh, Mac." Her voice was low with concern, husky in a way that made him think of warm summer nights and soft, tangled sheets.

"Don't you see?" she said. "It doesn't matter to me if you own all of Bear's Den, or a third, or none. I just don't want you to pin your hopes on people you can't count on."

He could explain it to her, he knew. Tell her about the three pubs he owned in Atlanta and the two in Dallas and the ones in Houston and Birmingham. Tell her that these days he was only letting the guys in on his deals because they'd been there for him when he was just getting started. But it didn't really matter right now whether he convinced her or not. What mattered was that she was admitting she cared about him.

He nodded his acceptance of her warning. "I'll keep that in mind—if you'll try to remember that first impressions aren't always accurate."

She smiled. "You mean you're not really a womanizing sex maniac who plays all night and sleeps all day?"

He loved her smile so much, he almost decided

to let her barb pass. "Only on the second and third Friday of every month."

He could see her mind clicking away.

"This *is* the second Friday of the month."

He waggled his eyebrows in his best Groucho Marx impression. "And the moon is full, and the night is young, and it's time for us to move on to the next step."

Her heart thrummed in wariness. "The next step?"

He winked and signaled for the check. "Ready?" He extended his hand.

Was she? She slipped her fingers into his, and images of those fingers skimming over her naked flesh flooded her mind. The next step. Oh, Lord.

"Kendra?"

She broke out of her daze. "Uh . . . that depends on what I'm supposed to be ready for?"

He smiled lazily, confidently. "Trust me, darlin'. You're gonna love it."

He helped her into her coat. Trust him? Strangely enough, she did. And had, almost from the beginning. Cold night air washed over her when they stepped out onto the sidewalk and moved slowly past darkened storefronts. She shivered, but not from the cold. *Was* she ready for the next step? she wondered. She looked at Mac, tall and handsome in the silvery moon glow, and her nerves quivered with excitement. Maybe. Maybe she should throw caution to the wind for once in her life and let Mac show her all the things he knew.

"Your carriage awaits, my lady."

She followed the sweep of his arm toward the

base of the hill. An old-fashioned sleigh, drawn by a single brown horse, was tied to a flickering streetlamp. The driver, dressed like a character from a Dickens novel, stood beside the horse, stroking its wide neck with a gloved hand.

Kendra smiled with delight. "Oh, Mac, is that for us?" At his nod, she hurried down the sidewalk, oblivious to the dusting of snow. "Can we go for a ride before he takes us back to the lodge?" She came to an abrupt halt when Mac wrapped a restraining hand around her arm.

His brown eyes glittered with moonlight and laughter. "Don't you think you'll need some help getting from here to there?" He glanced pointedly at the snow between them and the sleigh, then swung her up into his arms. "Can't have your toes suffering from frostbite."

She laughed at his foolishness but didn't argue. Her cheek rested against his broad shoulder, and her fingers tangled in his collar-length hair. It was so lush and silky.

"You did a lot of planning for tonight," she murmured. She looped a strand of hair around her finger. "Dinner in town, a car ride down the mountain, a sleigh to take us back . . ."

He shrugged. "A special night for a special lady."

"Special?" She tried not to read more into his words than his habitual teasing.

"It's only a few more hours till our third-night anniversary. I wanted to celebrate."

The night shadows cut his features into sharp relief. His profile was chiseled masculinity, his jaw as firm as if carved from a wall of granite. She could tell when he began to smile by the way the hard line softened.

"This isn't my first choice on how to celebrate a first third-night anniversary," he told her, "but it'll have to do."

"Oh? How would you prefer to spend it?"

His jaw tightened again when he glanced down at her. "In bed with you."

Her mouth popped open, but only air rushed out.

"You asked. But don't worry, darlin'." His tone was as placating as a mother's soothing an injured child. "I know I don't always get what I want. Right away."

It was that "right away" that worried her. All evening she'd been diving headfirst into swells of emotion, swimming into wave after wave of sensation. His touch, his scent, his honest hunger, had crashed over her until she was short of breath, drowning in wanting, and in danger of never returning to the shores of sanity.

He trudged to the sleigh in a silence broken only by the crunch of snow under his feet. And the pounding of her heart. She was sure even Mac could hear its booming thunder. Was she ready? Her body said yes, her mind said no, and her heart vacillated between excitement and panic.

"Yo, Mac. What's happenin', man?"

This from her Dickensian character? Kendra burst into giggles as they neared the driver.

"Evenin', Nico," Mac greeted the man. "Hope you haven't been waiting long."

"Nah." Nico stepped closer while Mac deposited Kendra in the front seat of the sleigh.

She was puzzled until Mac took the reins from the driver and climbed in next to her.

"Toss me that blanket, will you?"

Nico reached into the passenger seat and handed over a woolen lap robe.

"Meet you back at the lodge," Mac told Nico, after he'd finished settling the robe around Kendra. He gave the reins an experienced flick, and the sleigh glided forward.

"Hey, not too late, man. I gotta be home before dawn."

Mac laughed. "Don't worry, the doc here will see to that. She's the voice of reason. But have the lodge charge your tab to my room while you're waiting."

"You know it," the driver called after them.

"Nico's from Jersey," Mac explained. "He's quite a character."

She smiled.

"Nice guy, though." He flicked the reins again, and the sleigh moved faster. "I met him a couple of years ago when I was up here on a little business."

She didn't ask what kind of business that might have been. All she wanted was to feel the sleigh gliding beneath her, and Mac's body next to hers.

She slipped an arm through his and snuggled closer to his warmth. The snow glittered like diamonds in the moonlight, and stands of spruce loomed like dark sentinels.

"It's so beautiful," she said, lifting her face to the moon and the stars as the sleigh sped along the trail. She smiled with delight, wondering if in all her childhood dreams, she'd ever conjured up a fairy tale more perfect than this. Sweeping along in a diamond-dusted world beside a handsome prince.

Her heart ached with the realization that it was only make-believe. As soon as her vacation ended, she'd go back to her world of hospital corridors and cafeteria food.

She pushed away the face of reality with a sigh of longing. The horse's hooves beat a muted rhythm against the snow-packed ground. Mac wrapped his arm around her shoulders, pulling her even closer.

"Are you cold?" he asked, when she shivered with pleasure.

"Not a bit." She smiled, relishing everything from the crisp, frosty air to the warmth of Mac's arms and every star-filled nuance in between. She didn't know what magic, or madness, had conspired to make this night a farfetched combination of piggyback hiking and a blissful sleigh ride, but she'd never felt more alive.

"Oh, look!" she said, pointing to a tiny log cabin nestled in a grove of cedars. Golden light flickered at its windows.

"The cabin marks the end of the trail," Mac said. "It's a place to rest and warm up before starting back to town."

He guided the sleigh to a stop at the front of the building.

The view was breathtaking. The lights from Denning winked at them from below, and the moon lit the snowy trail winding through the darkened firs.

"I feel like we should be on a picture-postcard," she said softly. "Or in one of those glass paperweights that you turn upside down to make the snow swirl."

She could feel his gaze on her, quiet and intense. "*You* turn me upside down, darlin'. And inside out." He gave her a smile. "But if you turn me right side up, the snow wouldn't swirl, it would melt."

She tilted her face up, ready to take her chances with the snow . . . and with Mac. But he was already hopping out of the sleigh, offering her his hand to help her down.

"Let's go inside," he invited.

They found a burning pot-bellied stove, a woolen blanket spread picnic-style on the pine floor, and a chilled bottle of non-alcoholic champagne. A thermos, two glasses, and two foam cups sat beside a single, long stemmed rose.

She was incredulous. "What's all this?" She glanced around the tiny room, and saw a kerosene lamp that had provided the golden glow she'd seen from outside. She picked up the rose and stroked its velvet softness. "How did this—how did you do this?"

"Nico. I wanted us to have a nice, quiet evening." Mac said with a smile. "We *are* celebrating, you know."

He ushered her to the side of the blanket nearest the stove. "When you're warm enough we can open the champagne." He settled next to her and unscrewed the cap on the thermos. "I thought we'd better start with hot chocolate."

"You amaze me," she said. "When did you have time to arrange all this?"

"While you were primping." He poured steaming

chocolate into her cup. "You can get a lot done in two hours."

"I wasn't primping. I was washing my hair."

He gave her a frown. "Yeah? Well, some of us wish we could breathe through a shower cap long enough to wash for ten minutes, let alone two hours."

She laughed. "You could try a bath instead of a shower."

"Baths are for sissies. Unless it's a bath for two."

The chocolate wasn't as hot as the image that flashed through her mind.

He shrugged out of his jacket. "Are you warm enough yet?"

If he only knew! Nodding distracted, she placed her cup on the floor. He reached behind her to help her with her coat, leaning so near she could inhale his musky cologne along with his own subtle, masculine scent. She glanced up at him . . . and felt the world come to a slow, whirling stop.

His mouth was a whisper away from hers. Awareness spiced the room with the sharp tang of desire. She could feel the heat of his breath on her lips, see the way his eyes darkened in the lamplight.

"I can't look at you without wanting you," he whispered, turning her into the warmth of his arms. "And damn me if you have to, but I've been as good as I can be."

And he covered her mouth in a kiss that was as uncompromising as the darkest night, as all-consuming as the hottest fire.

That quickly, the last remnants of her control snapped. Like dry kindling, seasoned by years of loneliness, she went up in flames. She met his tongue thrust for thrust. She urged him with her mouth and her hands and her sighs to take more, to give more. And he did. He tasted, he sipped, he drank deeply. But it wasn't a seduction, Kendra realized dimly. The seduction had happened earlier—when he'd given her his laughter and his caring and his gentle understanding.

She reached out, her hand finding an anchor in the loose folds of his sweater where it settled near his waist. He shifted closer, letting his hands roam her back in long, restless sweeps. His heat warmed her through the layers of silk and wool separating them. She could feel the thunder of his heart matching hers. As if tempted by the same mesmerizing rhythm, his hand slipped between their bodies, touching the pulse in her neck, then tracing its way along her shoulder and under the lapel of her silk overblouse.

"Your skin is so soft," he told her, pushing away the material. "So much softer than this." The blouse slipped down her arm, baring her shoulders. He slid his hand under the strap of her bra and followed the curve of her neckline slowly, ever so slowly, to where it nestled against the swell of her breasts.

He skimmed his fingers over the soft, ivory skin that tingled with each featherlight touch. Pleasure raced through her in swirling undulations that settled low in her abdomen. She shivered when he gently nudged her strap lower, baring her rounded breast down to the slim crescent of pink that strained toward him, eager to feel his touch there too.

His breathing escalated. He lifted his gaze, and it tunneled into hers. "You do know what's happening here, don't you, Kendra? If we keep going, there'll be no stopping it."

She nodded, afraid if she spoke he would hear the emotion in her voice. She *knew* something was happening and it went beyond desire, beyond passion. She felt a . . . a change inside, a recklessness, a hunger—an emptiness that only Mac could fill.

He cupped her face with his hand. "You're sure this is what you want, darlin'?" He brushed his mouth over hers, and she could taste his hunger. "Please be sure."

"I am." Those words she could whisper. There was no denying what she wanted. The pebble-hard tips of her breasts would prove her a liar. Her soft gasp as he pressed his lips to her neck would tell him the truth. She wanted him. She wanted his touch and his taste and his magic. She wanted him so deep inside of her she wouldn't know where he ended and she began. It was frightening, this hunger.

He threaded his fingers through her hair and brought his mouth to hers. She could feel his passion in the rhythmic thrusts of his tongue as he lowered her to the soft woolen blanket.

Slowly, he let his heated gaze wander over her, lingering on her breasts, then her hips, then the long, supple line of her legs.

"So beautiful." His voice was husky. "I want to

touch you everywhere, see you everywhere, take every part of you and make it mine."

He started with her mouth, claiming it with the hungry thrusts of his tongue. He found new ways to delight, new treasures to seek. Stroking, plundering, sharing his bounty with each rhythmic thrust. And she found her treasures too. The passion-heated warmth of his body when she slipped her hands beneath his sweater. The taut skin along his lean waist. The dense hair that whorled across his muscled chest and arrowed beneath the waistband of his jeans.

She wasn't fully aware of when he slipped her shirt down her arms and unclasped her bra, completely baring her breasts to his gaze and his lips. She was only aware of the heat, the incredible heat of his hands and the burning flick of his tongue when he pulled a beaded nipple into his mouth and suckled her. She arched into the heat, into the pleasure, feeling each tug of his mouth shoot arrows of desire straight to the center of her need.

He pulled his sweater over his head, then covered her with the textured heat of his chest. She felt enveloped by warmth, cherished by the gentle rasp of his skin against hers. When he worked the button of her slacks, her breathing sharpened.

He lifted his gaze to meet hers. His eyes were hot, as hot as the need pulsing through her. His mouth covered hers in a kiss that was open and deep. And his fingers, his wicked, skillful fingers, slipped steadily lower, controlling and spurring the rhythm of her breathing.

"Mac." She sighed his name, trying to regain a drop of the control she'd so totally lost, but his hand slid lower, and he opened her to his touch. His fingers worked a sorcery on her that had her arching and trembling and eager to feel the full, warm length of him sliding inside her.

She reached for him, and it was his turn to sigh her name. His turn to tremble. He worked himself out of his jeans with quick, jerky movements, then carefully, slowly, eased her slacks down her hips. He lowered his head to kiss her stomach, her thighs, lingering to follow each caress of his lips with the moist tip of his tongue.

She sighed his name again, only this time with an urgency that matched the need building inside her. She almost whimpered when he moved from her, reaching for the jeans he'd slung hastily beside him. Her eyes widened when he dug into his pocket and pulled out a small flat packet.

She must have made some sound. His gaze darted to hers, then back to the packet in his hand.

"I haven't had irresponsible sex since I was seventeen years old, Kendra. And I wouldn't start with you. You mean too much to me."

She tried to feel reassured. "I guess it's good one of us was thinking ahead."

He brushed his fingers along the curve of her cheek. His eyes held gentle understanding. "It wasn't expectation, darlin'. It was only hope."

She saw the sincerity in his eyes, felt it in his touch. She took the packet from him and slowly, inexpertly, slid the protection over his strong, velvet length. He shuddered with her first touch and sighed with her next. Then, lacing his fingers through her hair, he lowered her beneath him.

"Do you know how crazy I am about you?" he whispered, worshiping her with his eyes. He praised her breasts with his mouth and his teeth and his tongue. He nipped, he soothed, he teased her and pleasured her until the urgency she'd felt before was only a faint echo of the need thrumming through her now.

She reached for him, wanting to feel him hard and strong within her. But he made her wait. He pushed her need even higher, stroking her with his hands, his tongue, murmuring to her, sighing with her when her own greedy hands played over his skin in feverish exploration.

And then he filled her, sliding deeper and deeper until she held all of him. Her breath hitched when he rocked against her, moving his hips in a slow, undulating rhythm. She sighed and rocked with him.

"Ah, darlin', . . . you feel so— Oh, yes. Just like that."

But soon *"that"* wasn't enough, for either of them. His hips moved faster as he thrust and withdrew, thrust and withdrew, stealing her breath and her heart with each powerful stroke. Her hands moved over his back, feeling the shifting pattern of his muscles as he surged into her, taking her with him in a mad, swirling dance. She leaped, she soared, burning hotter and hotter beneath the driving force of his body until the fire was out of control and she was exploding, shuddering, racing faster and faster into the white-hot flames of release.

Nine

Mac rolled to his side, cradling Kendra in his strong arms until she felt the world settle back into place. His chest rose and fell under her cheek. The rhythm of his breathing lulled her into a tranquillity that seemed blessed by the golden hue flickering from the hissing lamp. Her gaze strayed around the cabin. She wanted to remember everything about this night, even the cobwebs that hid in a quiet corner of the room.

She sighed and snuggled deeper into Mac's arms, smiling inwardly at the pleasure still sifting through her body. Perfect. That one word kept running through her head. Every touch, every sigh, every move had been perfect. And the way she felt now, lying in his arms . . . Even the chill sneaking up on her slowly cooling skin felt as if it should be there, like a gentle hand shaking her to awareness, making every moment sharper and clearer.

"Kendra? Darlin', are you cold?" Mac pushed

himself to a sitting position to pull some of the blanket around them. "Why didn't you say something?"

"I'm fine," she told him, watching the play of his muscles as he settled back beside her.

"That's what I thought the first time I saw you." His eyes sparkled with wicked humor. "I thought 'Mmm, mmm. Ain't she fine.'"

"Oh, sure." She smiled at his foolishness. "Me in my flannel nightgown and my argyle socks."

"A real fetchin' combination," he agreed, smiling. "But it was what was under the combination that interested me." He elaborated his point by drawing a finger along her exposed breast.

"Now, that I can believe."

"But," he said, seemingly fascinated by the way her nipple tautened when he traced a smaller and smaller circle toward it, "I wouldn't have cared what was under it if I hadn't liked what was over it."

"My coat?"

He sighed despairingly. "Your head, darlin'. That sassy-mouthed, flashing-eyed, beautiful head of yours."

She inhaled a deep breath when his tongue replaced his finger. "You—oh! . . . You liked my mouth?"

He blew gently on her tongue-dampened nipple, and she could feel it drawing into a tighter bead.

"I love your mouth." He leaned up to give her lips a soft, lingering kiss. "And your eyes." He kissed each lid. "And this cute freckle right . . . here."

She shivered when he pressed his moist lips to

the sensitive skin just above the swell of her breast.

"And I love the soft little sounds you make whenever I'm kissing you . . . like this . . ."

His mouth closed over her nipple, and she knew she was making those sounds, but she couldn't help it. And she didn't want to. She wanted him to know how much she loved what he was doing to her. She loved his mouth, and his hands, and the way he touched her. She loved his scent and his taste and the sweet things he whispered, and his tenderness and his compassion and— Oh, Lord. She stiffened. What if she loved *him*?

"What? What?" Mac looked up at her with anxious concern. "Did I hurt you?"

She stared numbly into his soft brown eyes. Could she actually have gone and fallen in love with him?

"Kendra? Darlin'?"

"No, no, of course not."

"Then what?"

"The—the floor," she lied, grasping at anything that would cover the truth. "It's—"

"Damn!" He rolled quickly, pulling her over onto his chest. "I'm sorry, darlin'." He smoothed a hand down her back to the indentation above her hips. "Are you sore?"

She shook her head, but his gentle concern was like a knife cutting into her already tender feelings. How could she have deluded herself into thinking the emotions swirling through her had been due to the moonlight or the night or the magic or anything other than Mac? She buried her face in the curve of his neck. She was such a fool. Falling in love—for the first time in her life—with a man she'd known only three days. A man who she knew—she *knew*—wasn't any more serious about her than he was about his games or his teasing or his stupid stitches.

She squeezed back a tear. She would not fall apart, she insisted, sniffing. She had no one to blame but herself. Mac couldn't help it if he was wonderful and handsome and gentle and caring. He hadn't pretended to be anything other than what he was, while she . . . she'd let herself act as if she were as reckless and devil-may-care as he. And she was nothing like that. Never had been. Never would be. The minute she set foot back in St. Louis, she'd slip out of her vacation dream and turn into sensible, dependable, responsible Dr. Kendra Davis.

"Darlin'?" Mac's voice intruded on her self-pity. "You're not cryin' or anything, are you?"

She looked up, wanting to prove to him and to herself that she wasn't. "No. I was just thinking." She pasted on a brilliant smile. "We haven't had our champagne yet."

"And we're not going to."

"But—"

"Not till we get back to the lodge and something a lot softer for us to lie on." He lifted them both into a sitting position."

"Us?" She inquired archly.

His smile was devilishly wicked and boyishly sweet. "Hope, darlin', hope."

If all hopes were fulfilled as easily as Mac's, Kendra thought, propping herself more comfortably in his bed, there would be world peace and universal wealth. She'd had every intention of coming back to the lodge, giving him a good-night kiss, and going back to her room to think. She needed to think. But then he'd kissed her in the elevator, and then in the hall, and then, well— she glanced ruefully down at the tangled bedding—she'd forgotten all about thinking.

She had to admit, no one had ever made her forget herself so completely before. Not even the one other man she'd let into her life and into her bed. He'd been everything she'd thought she wanted: steady, reliable, dependable. Everything. But she hadn't loved him. As hard as she'd tried, she just hadn't loved him.

She looked at Mac, standing arrogantly naked before the low chest of drawers while he worked at opening the champagne bottle. The muscles in his back shifted rhythmically as he tore the foil off the cork. Her heart constricted in a grip of love so strong it was painful. She hadn't wanted to love him. She hadn't even considered it a danger. And now . . .

"I've got it," Mac called as the cork gave way.

He threaded his fingers between the stems of two tulip glasses and carried them and the bottle back to the bed. The mattress sank when he settled beside her, dislodging the sheet she'd tucked cozily around her. She grabbed it and anchored it under her arms.

"Ah, darlin', don't cover yourself up. I know this really fun game that has to do with champagne. . . ."

She gave him a reproving frown. "The thought of

cold liquid on various parts of my anatomy doesn't thrill me at all."

He cocked his head. "You've played that game before?"

"No. I just know how your mind works."

"Good." He handed her a glass and filled it. "I sort of don't like the idea of your playing it with someone else."

That surprised her. And pleased her. She'd never imagined Mac to be the jealous type.

He filled his own glass and clinked it against hers. "Happy third-night anniversary, darlin'."

She smiled and started to take a sip, but he stopped her.

"No. Not like that." He set the bottle on the floor, then linked an arm through hers. "Like this."

She held his gaze and lifted her glass, not recognizing the devilry in his eyes until it was too late. The cold liquid had barely dampened her mouth when he "accidentally" jarred her arm, drizzling champagne over her breasts. "Mac!" She gasped, trying to catch her breath against the shocking chill.

"Good grief." His dimples danced happily. "Now, how did that happen?"

"You rat!" She mopped at her chest with a corner of the sheet.

"Hey, don't be wasting it."

He leaned over to help her, but she pushed his face away. "Oh, no, you don't, buster." Without a second thought, she dumped what was left of her drink over his chest.

"Geez!" He sucked in a breath. "That's cold!"

His shocked outrage made her giggle. "Now,

how do you suppose that happened?" she mimicked, trying not to laugh too hard.

Carefully, too carefully, he set his glass on the nightstand. Then he crooked his finger. "Come here, you little devil."

"You had that coming, Mac." She pressed her lips closed against the laughter trying to break free. "You know you did."

His dimples flashed at her. "Yes, ma'am, I did. And now I want to thank you for teaching me such a well-deserved lesson."

She shook her head, inching away.

He nodded, inching closer.

He lunged. She rolled. He caught her by the waist and hauled her up against him. The devil danced like lightning in his eyes. She tried to tickle her way to freedom, and laughter rolled out of him like booming thunder.

"Stop that. Stop—Kendra—stop!

He pinned her beneath him, locking her hands safely above her head. His chest covered hers. His stomach jumped with the laughter still bubbling there. He smiled, wide and fully.

"God, I love you, you crazy, crazy woman."

For a heart-catching moment she thought he might be serious, but the thought dissipated like a puff of smoke. She smiled up at him. "There's only one candidate for the nut house in this room, buddy. And it's not me."

"If I go, you go. You're just as bad as I am."

She squirmed against him. "I am not."

"Uh-oh. The lady doth protest too much. That's a sure sign."

She looked up at him, suddenly finding the

situation curiously hurtful. All her life she'd
wished she were something other than what she
was, and all her life she'd had to fight that wish.
Finally she had accepted that she would never be
easygoing, or free-spirited or any of those things
she so admired in others. Maybe she had been a
little less reserved than usual these past few days.
Well, okay, a lot less reserved. But it was only
because of Mac. And it hurt to think that maybe
he liked her only because he saw her as something other than what she really was.

"You know, I'm not usually so . . ."

"Abandoned?" he suggested, taking a little sip
from her lips.

For the first time, she didn't feel like kissing him
back: She wanted him to listen to her.

"I'm not like that," she insisted.

He grinned playfully. "Darlin', you're the most
abandoned, generous woman I know."

"No, I'm not." This wasn't fun anymore, and,
like an animal needing privacy to lick its wounds,
she wanted to turn away from him. But first she
wanted him to face the truth.

"You know the only reason I got a little silly was
because I—"

He touched his lips to hers again.

". . . because I . . ." Words were difficult to
find. "Because . . ."

"You're as crazy as I am," he teased.

"Mac." She twisted her hands free. "I'm not
abandoned, and I'm not crazy, and you know it."

Mac lifted himself off her, suddenly realizing she
wasn't playing anymore.

He touched a finger to the tear seeping out of

her eye. He'd never thought a tiny drop of water could hurt so much. "Darlin', what did I do?" He grabbed her wrists, looking for signs that he'd been too forceful in his play. He scanned her body. Her skin was as flawless and beautiful as always.

"You're not listening to me," she said raggedly. "You're not hearing me."

He was completely lost. "Not hearing what? I don't understand what's happening here."

Another tear slipped down her cheek. She swiped at it angrily.

"No, you don't." Her voice shook. "You don't understand that you're talking about somebody else. You're not talking about me."

"I wasn't talking about anyone but you, Kendra. I wasn't playing with, or making love with, or falling in love with anyone but you."

A fresh surge of tears leaked out of her eyes. "You can't love me!" she sobbed. "You don't even know me."

A spark of understanding brightened the darkness. "I know it's only been three days, darlin', but we've spent almost every minute of those three days together. That's more hours then lots of people spend in six weeks of regular dating. People can fall in love in a month or two. Sure, there are things we'll have to learn about each other. But we already know what's important."

She shook her head. "No, we don't. I hardly know you, and you"—-more tears—"don't know me at all."

He persevered. "Sure, I don't know what kind of ice cream you like, or your favorite kind of music, or whether you prefer sitcoms or dramas. But I promise I won't stop loving you because you like strawberry better than chocolate, or jazz instead of country-western." He scooted closer to her. "And I'd rather make love with you than watch TV anyway."

She let him get close enough to put an arm around her. "I know what counts, Kendra. I know how good you are, and how caring. I know we laugh together, and we burn up the bed together, and I know I'd rather cut out my heart than hurt you."

She shook her head and wiped at her tears.

"Oh, Mac. I wish it were true. I really, really do."

"It is, darlin'. It is."

She looked up at him with those big, shimmering eyes, and he felt them pulling at his emotions.

She sighed and lifted her hand, then let it fall back into her lap. He might have taken it as a gesture of defeat, but he knew she hadn't given up the battle yet. Poor baby. She just didn't understand. The war was over. The good guys had won.

"You probably think it would be like that all the time," she said, launching her new offensive. "You probably think I make it a matter of routine to fall into bed with some guy I've only known for three days."

"I'm not *some* guy, Kendra. I'm the guy who loves you. And, no, I don't think that."

"Well, you'd better not." She lifted her chin. "I've had one affair in my whole life. One."

He nodded his acceptance, even though he wasn't crazy about the thought of her with anyone else. But he knew she'd never be with anyone else ever again, so he didn't let himself think about it.

"And you probably think I'm used to sleigh rides and champagne and . . . and all this. But I'm not. I can't be a party girl all the time, Mac. If you could see me back in St. Louis, you'd know what I mean."

Her expression was so earnest and he wanted to kiss her so badly that he made himself move away from her. He propped himself against the headboard and crossed his arms. He remembered then, when he felt his own skin beneath him, that he was naked. And so was she.

He pulled the sheet up to cover his growing awareness and listened patiently while she tried to explain.

"This is a vacation, for heaven's sake." She gestured around the room. "I'd never do any of these things if I weren't on vacation. We had a bargain, remember? We were going to show each other the error of our ways. And I was trying to live up to it. I'd never in my wildest dreams take a piggyback ride in St. Louis, I don't do things like that. Do you understand now? You think you love somebody, Mac, but that somebody doesn't exist except right here, right now."

"She does exist," he insisted. "And she always has."

At her frustrated sigh, he shot her a look he'd often used in settling down his brothers and sisters. He'd learned that look from his mom. It was lethal. And it worked with Kendra. She didn't say another word, even though he knew she was dying to.

"You haven't been anything with me except what you are. I know you haven't had much fun in your life. Hell, darlin', you haven't had a chance. You've been mother and father to your sister. You've put yourself through medical school. You've never even had a vacation before. When were you supposed to play? While your mom was dying or your dad was drinking?"

He sat up, leaning close so she could see that he meant every word.

"You've done the things you've done these past few days because, down deep in that beautiful body of yours, you wanted to. And if you try to tell me you're only in this bed because of some damned bargain, we'll both know you're lying. You're here because you love me. Or if you don't, you're so damn close you don't have far to fall. And I mean for you to fall. All the way, darlin'. As totally and completely as I have."

She was speechless. For the first time in her life, she was totally speechless. She ran a hand through her hair, waiting for something to come to mind. He was wrong. He had to be wrong. Not about the bed part. She'd admit to that. But the rest of it was all crazy. Wasn't it? She rubbed her temples. How could he love her? They were so different. But, wait—she loved him, didn't she? Yes, her heart said. It was just that in her mind, she knew it couldn't work. Oh, Lord. She scrubbed her face with her hands. She was so confused.

"Come here, darlin'."

She peeked at him between her fingers. How could he look so calm? Didn't he know this was serious stuff they were playing with? Didn't he know her heart was at stake here?"

"This isn't going to work, Mac." The fact that she was a basket case and he looked perfectly relaxed was all the proof she needed.

He smiled reproachfully. "It'll work. You just have to give it a chance. Now, why don't you come here and let me hold you."

She shook her head. "I'm going to my room. I need to think." And she needed to call Leslie. Good grief, she probably even needed a drink.

"Okay. Fine. Whatever you say."

She knew she'd lost it then. She wanted to go to her room, but he didn't have to agree so easily. "Well, okay, then," she muttered.

He sat up and rummaged around on the floor.

"What are you doing?"

"Looking for my clothes." He lifted his hand. Her panties were hooked over his index finger. "This will probably fit you better than it will me."

She took the scrap of silk and slipped it on. "You don't need to walk me down the hall, Mac. It's perfectly safe."

"I know." He found his underwear. "But whither though goest . . ." He smiled sweetly.

"Really, Mac. I'll be fine."

"Darlin', you're gonna be finer than you can possibly imagine, 'cause I'm gonna be stuck to you like a tick on a dog. If you think I'm about to let you walk down that hall and shut the door between us, you've got another think comin'." He shoved his legs into his navy-blue briefs. "You want to go to your room? Fine. I can sleep there as well as I can here. But wherever you are, that's where I am. Got it?"

Her mouth popped open, then snapped shut.

"You have something you want to say, Kendra?"
She shook her head.

"Good. I think we've done enough talking for one night. Anything that needs clarifying we can go over in the morning." He crawled back into bed and held the cover open for her. "Now, are you gonna come here, or what?"

She'd known from the moment he nudged her out of bed the next morning that Mac wasn't going to clarify a thing. He was just going to "fun" her to death. Kendra looked down the steep slope of the mountain crisscrossed with tracks from earlier skiers and gulped.

"You're sure I can do this?" she asked, knowing there was no way in hell.

"It's the same experience level as the last one," he told her. Again. "It's just a different trail."

"I know. And I'm sure I'll experience just as many falls."

"Kendra, Kendra, Kendra." He shook his head. "That's not the right attitude. It's *thrills*, darlin'. 'I'm sure I'll experience just as many *thrills*.' But, hey, don't let me sway you one way or the other. The decision is all yours."

A young boy, not more than nine or ten years old, angled toward them from the lift.

"S'cuse me," he muttered before he launched himself over the rim and down the trail. His thin legs wobbled. His skis seemed to be trying to make an escape, each one sliding in a different direction, but the boy remained upright until he was out of sight.

Kendra sighed. "Okay. I know. If he can do it, I can do it." She gritted her teeth and shoved off with her poles.

Her teeth were still gritted when she reached the bottom of the slope, but now it was from the smile plastered on her face.

"That was great, darlin'." Mac came to a graceful stop beside her, wearing a smile that matched hers. "You did great."

"I know," she said, laughing. "Not one fall!"

"You're gonna be skiing better than me by the end of the day."

"Oh, right. And you'll be doing brain surgery."

She couldn't see behind his reflecting sunglasses, but she knew his eyes were dancing. His dimples slashed down his cheeks in bold, sexy strokes. His straight teeth gleamed white in the sunlight. His wind-tossed hair shifted in a gentle breeze. She had an overpowering urge to twine her fingers through his hair, to run the tip of her tongue over the gentle curve of his lips.

Even as she thought it, his mouth lowered to hers and he gave her a brushing kiss that ended almost before it began. "I love it when you get sassy," he told her.

His smile deepened, and her heart skipped in a jerky beat that was half despair, half delight. There it was again. That four-letter word. Love. She'd lain awake in his arms and thought and worried and come to no sound conclusions about anything. It was so soon, so fast.

"You know, Kendra, I think that's about the hundredth time I've told you I love you in one way or another. It would sure help my ego out if you'd admit that you love me too." He tilted her chin up and smiled that wicked smile. "Just one little 'I love you' for good ol' Mac? Just one?"

"I thought we were supposed to talk about this today."

He grinned his cocky grin. "We are talking. I've said my part, now it's time for you to say yours."

"Mac . . . I—" Fear clenched her heart.

"It's not so hard. Let me show you. 'I—Well, come on—'I' . . ."

"I," she repeated doubtfully.

"'Love' . . ."

"Love." It wasn't quite as bad as she'd thought it would be.

"'You' . . ."

"Y—"

"Mac! Hey, Mac! Thank the good Lord I found you." Skip schussed to a stop beside them. Kendra hadn't heard Mac swear quite so vilely since he'd been suffering from his injury.

"You have the worst damn timin'," he all but yelled. "What do you want, Skip?"

"Well, excuse me for living. But I thought you'd want to know that Terry just got a call from Susie's sister. Susie's in the hospital."

Kendra felt Mac's instant tension. "What's wrong with her? Is she all right?"

"They think it might be a heart attack."

"Oh, Lord." Mac swiped a hand over his face. "How's Terry holding up?"

"He's a basket case. The plane will be ready when we get to the airport. You've got just enough time to grab your gear."

Kendra knew it was selfish, she knew it was heartless, but all she could think was, that's it. It's over. He'll get on a plane and fly out of my life, and I'll never see him again.

He turned toward her.

"Darlin'—"

"I know," she interrupted. "You've got to go." Her voice quivered. "Susie's your best girl, isn't she? You have to go."

"Come with me."

Her heart stopped. "What?"

"Come with me, Kendra. We'll talk. You said yourself we need to talk. Come with me. We'll talk till we're blue in the face."

"Mac, I—" she didn't know what to say. She could hear the panic in her voice, feel it pounding through her heart. Her mind, so confident when it came to making choices based on information and experience, reeled in confusion. How could she go? How could she not? The thought of saying good bye right now was not to be borne. But how could she go? She'd need to pack and call home and . . . "I couldn't be ready fast enough, Mac," she said numbly.

He took her arm and propelled her toward the lodge.

"You've never seen anyone pack until you've seen me. I can have you out of that room in ten minutes flat."

"But I need to—"

"And I need you, darlin'. I need you with me. I hate to ruin your vacation, but I'll make it up to you, I promise."

She closed her eyes, uncertain if the thudding

in her heart was due to fear or excitement. She wasn't certain if she was taking a step forward or only prolonging the inevitable. But did she really have a choice? The bottom line was, he needed her. How could she say no to that?

Ten

"It's okay, Kendra. We're down."

Kendra sighed and opened her eyes cautiously. She could feel the Learjet decelerating as it taxied toward the jetport. Still, in spite of the knowledge that they were safely on ground, she felt a tight flutter of anxiety low in her stomach. "I'm sorry. I don't know what's the matter with me."

Mac squeezed her hand. "Don't worry about it. That turbulence back there just upset your stomach."

"Maybe so." But she didn't think that was it. The flutters had started the moment she'd seen the sleek jet sitting outside the hangar at the airport. "I survived that puddle-jumper from Denver," she mused, "and this"—she glanced around the luxurious cabin—"is a far cry from that piece of tin in the middle of a snowstorm."

He laughed. "That it is, darlin'. We'd still be in

the air three hours from now if we'd tried to fly home in a twin-engine Cessna."

"And we'd still be worrying about Susie."

He gave her hand another squeeze. "Thank God for in-flight phones. And thank God Susie's gonna be all right. I don't know what Terry would have done if it had turned out to be a heart attack instead of that—that gas stuff."

"Acute gastritis is very painful and can be quite serious."

Mac grimaced. "Well, don't tell Terry that. He's had about all he can handle for one day."

"You care a lot for Terry and his wife, don't you?"

She saw tenderness in his eyes as he cleared his throat. "Yeah. I'd probably be the mechanic my father wanted if it weren't for Terry. He gave me my first job in the restaurant business and helped me get my first bank loan. And Susie . . . well, I think Susie probably talked him into it."

"So that's how you got involved with 'the boys'?"

"Yep."

He unbuckled his seat belt, and Kendra realized the plane had stopped.

"Terry?" Mac leaned across the aisle and placed his hand on the other man's arm. "Give Susie a kiss for me and tell her we'll be up to see her tomorrow. Kendra's not feeling so hot, so I'm gonna take her home."

"I'm fine now," she objected.

"You go on and rest a bit, honey," Terry urged. "To tell you the truth, I'd kind of like to be alone with Susie for a bit. That fool sister of hers is gonna get a chewing out for scarin' me half to death, but I gotta get Susie's okay first." He winked.

Kendra shared his smile. "I understand."

"Take good care of this little filly now, Mac. We can use a doctor in the family." He started toward the exit.

Kendra stared at Mac. "You're related to them?"

"Only in spirit. Over the years we've all sort of become family to each other."

He helped her out of her seat and off the plane. Atlanta was colder than Kendra had expected, reminding her of St. Louis and displacing the image she'd had of sprawling Southern mansions with oak-lined drives.

"I'm parked over there." Mac nodded to a private area just beyond the jetport. "You want to wait here and I'll come around for you and the luggage?"

She shook her head, suddenly unwilling to let him out of her sight. That sensation of unease was back, and she recognized it for what it was—fear. Fear of losing what they'd shared in Colorado, fear of facing reality and finding it too intrusive. "There's no need," she said quickly. "We've just got the three suitcases. We can carry them."

He nodded, then helped the pilot retrieve the luggage from the cargo hold before leading her across the parking lot. When they stopped beside a late-model pickup truck and he tossed the luggage into the bed, Kendra's stomach settled a bit. A truck was more in keeping with the image she had of Mac than Learjets. A pickup truck, a small house in a modest residential area, and maybe a dog. She liked those images.

And she liked the lingering kiss he gave her after they were settled in the truck. She welcomed his lips and the velvet rasp of his tongue. She felt safe again, more secure, as she tasted his familiar essence.

"Welcome to Atlanta, darlin'." He dropped another kiss on her lips. "You think you'll like it here?"

"You might give me a chance to see a bit more of it than a parking lot before I make my decision."

He grinned and started the truck. "I'll give you a scenic tour on the way home." He glanced at her. "But do you think it would upset your stomach if we stopped and got something to eat first? I don't know about you, but I'm starved."

The thought of food produced a slight grumbling of hunger pains. "Food sounds good."

"You're sure?"

She nodded. "I guess it was the turbulence after all."

"Good. We can eat, do a little sightseeing, and be home by—oh, seven-thirty." His gaze traveled over her in slow, sizzling degrees while he grinned like the devil who'd just bought a lost soul. "That'll give us more time for *talking* tonight."

She gave him a reproving frown. "We *will* talk, Mac."

"Yes, ma'am. I promised, didn't I?"

"Yes." She knew how easily promises were broken.

"We can talk now, if you want," Mac said, making her feel a start of guilt. "How 'bout kids? That's a pretty important subject. I'd like a couple of kids. But I think we should have some time on our own together first." He glanced at her as if to insure she agreed. Apparently satisfied with the stunned look on her face, he rambled on. "We probably shouldn't wait more than a couple of years for the first one, though. My mother wants grandchildren." He glanced at her again. "And the old biological clock is ticking, you know."

Her mouth popped open. "Mac . . ."

"Then there's the subject of careers. I guess that's pretty much cut-and-dried for us. You have yours, I have mine. The important thing about that is—"

"Mac?"

"—making sure we prioritize our time. Can't let the jobs cut into the marriage."

"Mac? What are you doing?"

He glanced in his side mirror as he eased the truck into expressway traffic. "Talking. As for finances—I'll handle those if you don't mind. I'm pretty good at it. And I'll help around the house. My mom made sure all us boys—"

"Mac!" Her heart was kicking up such a ruckus, she knew what a patient going into cardiac arrest felt like.

He shot her a look so innocent that she knew he knew exactly what he was doing. "I thought you wanted to talk," he complained.

"Talk is supposed to be an exchange of ideas. Not a soliloquy on the dos and don'ts of—of marriage."

He nodded. "And those are my ideas about some stuff. What are yours?"

She was forced to admit, "In principle, I agree with you."

"Okay. Discounting principles, what don't you agree with?"

She felt a twinge of panic. This was all too unreal. "I . . . I think married people should share financial decisions," she hedged.

"So do I." He whipped the truck into an exit lane.

"What else?"

"Well, I . . . I guess I pretty much agree with everything else. In principle."

He beamed. "Good. See how compatible we are?"

"You make me crazy," she said. "And you snore."

He did a double take, then laughed. "I'll have my deviated septum fixed."

"What if *I* snore?"

His gaze flowed over her like hot smoke. "You don't."

Her breath hitched in a rush of desire as she contemplated how he'd discovered that. The same way she'd found out he did snore. They'd slept together, wrapped in each other's arms, exhausted and sated. Her breasts tingled at the memory of their lovemaking. And her heart ached with the knowledge that their time together was almost over.

The truck made a sharp turn, then coasted to a stop. She looked out the window. She could see houses lining the streets behind a smattering of small businesses that dotted the main thoroughfare. The area stirred memories of home. Home without Mac? A surge of panic pummeled her imagination. Maybe he could come back to St.

Louis with her. He could spend a few days, and they could . . . they could . . . what? Watch TV because she'd be too tired to go out. Or he could hang around the hospital and wait for the occasional slack time so they could steal a few kisses. Big thrill. What could she offer Mac in St. Louis besides the mundane humdrum of her life? She couldn't offer him the kind of fun he liked. She couldn't play all night and work all day. She couldn't offer him anything but her heart, and that wouldn't be enough. It hadn't been enough to keep her mother from dying or her father from drinking or Bridgett from leaving, and it wouldn't be enough to keep Mac.

She hadn't realized how far her mind had strayed until the cold air hit her as Mac opened her door. His hand, warm and solid, closed over hers as he helped her from the truck.

"Hang on a minute, darlin', while I stow the luggage in the cab." His movements were quick and easy. "I hope you don't mind more of the same as last night," he said, taking her hand again to lead her toward the restaurant. "But I know we can get good service here." His mouth twitched. "And the price is right."

For the first time, she paid attention to the restaurant they were approaching. The old English architecture. The smoke-glass doors. She glanced at the sign over the entrance and saw O'CONNER'S CORNER. She was totally confused. "What . . . ?"

"This is the first one we built," he explained, as if she weren't about to fall into a dead faint.

"Business isn't as good here as at some of the others, but it's—"

"Others?"

He looked too smug as he pushed open the front door. "Yeah. You didn't think Bear's Den was the only one, did you?"

"I—I—" How could she tell him she hadn't completely believed him about Bear's Den, much less thought there would be any other pubs?

His expression didn't reveal his thoughts, but Kendra knew he'd guessed what she thought. And he'd let her think it.

No, she realized, he hadn't let her. She'd made her own assumptions, despite what he'd tried to tell her. Her stomach got that tight, clenching feeling again. What else had she assumed? What other misconceptions did she nurse?

He led her past the entry directly into the dining area. A waitress nodded to them from a nearby table.

"How many other restaurants are there?" Kendra asked quietly.

He waited until they were seated before he answered. "Eight."

The breath whooshed out of her. "Eight?" Her voice shook a little. "They must keep you pretty busy."

He shrugged. "I used to work twenty-four hours a day, seven days a week. But I'm finally at a point where I don't have to spend every minute worrying or working. I've got managers for that. And accountants. Now I just sort of keep an eye on things."

She nodded in dawning comprehension. "Like an occasional visit to Colorado."

"And Texas. And Alabama."

Kendra felt her spirits sinking lower and lower as her stomach knotted tighter and tighter. She tried to stop the downward spiral of her thoughts, but every time she looked at Mac she felt as if she were seeing him for the first time.

And perhaps she was. All of her old conceptions were rapidly fading. She'd come to Atlanta wanting to hold on to the dream for a little while longer. But with each passing moment, she could feel it slipping further and further away.

She was slipping further and further away. Mac could feel it with each ticking heartbeat. He looked at Kendra standing silently beside him in the elevator as it zipped up to his apartment. Despite the smile she gave him, he could see her tension mounting. Why, dammit? He racked his brain. Why?

He didn't understand what was happening here. He'd thought when he brought her to Atlanta she'd see that what they shared wasn't a vacation dream, as she'd insisted. He'd thought she'd see that his life was not that different from hers, that he understood about commitment and responsibility. But it wasn't working. Why?

She'd seemed okay on the way to the pub, he remembered. They'd talked, laughed. Then at dinner—no, before dinner—when she'd realized he owned O'Conner's Corner, she'd started to . . .

A seed of understanding grew. A seed that tasted bitter. He didn't want to believe that everything was backfiring on him. She couldn't possibly think that . . . ? No. She wouldn't think that just because he was more financially secure than she'd thought, that he was any different, or felt any differently about her. No. He shrugged off the idea. Maybe she was only tired, as she'd said. Maybe . . .

The elevator doors opened and he broke off his mental debate to gather up the luggage and lead the way to his apartment. He unlocked the door and gestured her in. Everything would be okay, he assured himself. They'd relax, talk, get back to the way things were.

Kendra stepped hesitantly into the vestibule of Mac's apartment, only to stop and stare, wide-eyed, around the plush penthouse. Glass-and-bronze, muted walls, vast abstract paintings, and plush furniture resting on an equally plush carpet met her gaze. "You live here?" she asked, knowing it was a foolish question. But she couldn't make the room fit with the man who'd played football in his hotel room and cheated at cards and who'd made her laugh and sigh and moan with pleasure.

He cocked his head. "Don't sound so surprised, darlin'." His suede-soft voice sounded more like rough corduroy as he switched on the recessed ceiling lights. "I might think you didn't like it or something."

"Oh, I like it." The richness of the room was softened by hanging plants and colored throw pillows. An étagère housed a tasteful arrangement of books and crystal. "I just hadn't pictured any-thing quite like this."

He smiled. "You pictured where I'd live?"

She tried to smile back, but she could feel the dullness in it. Her heart was slowly plummeting. Every preconceived notion she'd had of Mac was so totally different from reality, she wondered how she could have imagined for a moment that she'd known him at all.

The warm, fuzzy pictures she'd painted had been of mismatched furniture and forgotten beer cans. Of sports magazines strewn across a coffee table and a favorite T-shirt left dangling from a doorknob.

None of her images fit. Each carefully selected object in the room was a tangible rift in the emotional portrait she'd painted of Mac, a painful reminder that her time with him was an illusion. And illusions were only temporary.

"I'd pictured something a little different," she told him, trying to brighten her smile.

But he wasn't fooled. She could see it in the way he studied her. His eyes were like quiet storms, dark and cloudy, with no hint of thunder or lightning. Yet.

"It's just an apartment, Kendra. Decorated by a professional. Lived in by a bachelor. It's a reflec-tion of my bank account, darlin', not my soul." He looked from her to the ivory-hued walls and back again. "It's supposed to be impressive, not intim-idating."

"It's beautiful, Mac." She wandered over to the étagère and picked up an exquisite vase. It wasn't that she minded that Mac had money. It was just that she'd thought him a dreamer, and here was visible proof that his dreams had already come true. What could she possibly offer this man that he didn't already have?

"I'm sorry if I gave you the wrong impression." She carefully replaced the vase. "It's just that—" Her voice caught. She tried to smile, but she couldn't. Being foolish wasn't something she could smile about. "I'm tired. But tiredness is no excuse for rudeness."

"You weren't being rude." He gave her a reassuring smile. "It's not required that you ooh and ahh."

"But I—"

"Don't worry about it," he said, straddling the arm of the sofa. "It's been a hectic day, and we're both tired. What we need is a chance to kick back and relax. How would you feel about a nice hot shower, and a quiet night in front of the TV? Tomorrow we can go see Susie and then tour a few more sights. Go someplace really nice for dinner. I can see if I can get reservations at The Abbey or—"

"Mac." She couldn't let him go on making plans that wouldn't happen. "Mac, we won't have time for all that. I have to go home tomorrow."

"What?"

The room grew so quiet, she could have sworn he'd hear the confused pounding of her heart. He shook his head, looking at her with frank disbelief.

"When did you decide this?" he asked.

"What do you mean, decide?"

"Come on, Kendra. Do you think I can't tell there's something going on here?" He levered himself off the couch and crossed the room, standing so near she could detect the lingering scent of the cologne he'd put on that morning. "You're tense as a cat under a rocker," he said, kneading her shoulders in a slow, even rhythm. "What's got you so shook that you want to hightail it out of here?"

"I . . . I'm not hightailing. I'm due back at the hospital the day after tomorrow."

"So call in and tell them you're taking a few more days."

"I can't do that." She lifted her gaze to his. "My vacation is over Monday."

He stopped kneading. "Come on, darlin'. Don't be like this. We need some time. . . ."

She stiffened, focusing on the most telling of his words. "Be like what, Mac?" she asked quietly, pulling free from his touch. "Like myself?" She pushed back the wave of pain rushing at her. "I tried to tell you," she reminded him. "I told you I wasn't the woman you thought I was. This is me, Mac. I'm not spontaneous, and I'm not abandoned. I'm no more like I was in Colorado than you are."

He stood perfectly still. "What are you talking about? We're the same two people we were yesterday."

She shook her head. "It's all different now, isn't it? You feel it too. That's why you said 'Don't be like this.' You want me to be the way I was, and I can't."

"That's not what I meant. I only meant we need more time together. I want you to—"

"Forget about my responsibilities in St. Louis and prolong my vacation?" she finished for him.

His gaze drilled into hers. "I'm talking about a

hell of a lot more than a vacation, Kendra, and you know it. I'm in love with you. That means I want the whole ball of wax. Marriage. Kids. The whole nine yards."

Her heart skidded to a stop, then leaped to a pounding start. She took a deep breath and tried to grapple with the emotions ripping through her, but it couldn't be done. Everything was racing too fast, too hard.

"Don't do this, Mac. Please don't do this."

"Do what?" he asked. He was pushing, he knew. He could hear the quaver in her voice, see the panic in her eyes. But he couldn't stop. It would be like asking himself to stop breathing. "What don't you want me to do? Tell you how I feel? Tell you what I want?"

"Don't try to force me into a decision I'm not ready to make."

He paced away a step to stop himself from dragging her into his arms. "When will you be ready? In six weeks, six months, six years? How much time will it take for you to decide that this is the real thing? That this is for keeps?" He choked back a roar of pure frustration. "But we don't have any more time, do we, darlin'? You're not gonna give us any more time."

"We have tonight."

He felt as if he'd been poleaxed. For a mind-numbing moment, his emotions went blank, then flared anew in a rush of disbelief.

"Is that all you want?" he asked carefully. "One more night?"

"It's all we have."

He let his temper free. "I stopped being anyone's

'one more night' a long time ago, Kendra. And I'm not gonna be that for you, no matter how much I love you."

"Mac, I—" What could she say? That she wished there could be more? But what good would wishing do? She'd offered him what she could, but it wasn't enough. "Maybe I should call and see if I can get a flight to St. Louis tonight."

He held her gaze, his golden brown eyes giving away nothing except the fire of anger. "If that's what you want," he said finally.

It wasn't. She wanted him to take her in his arms and turn away the rest of the world. But tomorrow would come, and the end would be the same. She blinked back her tears of regret and longing and nodded. "I think it would be best."

Mac insisted on driving her to the airport. He was, after all, a Southern gentleman. The ride was so rife with unresolved tension that Kendra could feel it crowding the small pickup cab. Mac's stony silence was in stark contrast to his usually flippant tongue. The tight set of his jaw, the controlled aggression that whipped the truck down the freeway, squeezed her heart.

When they pulled into the airport parking area, Kendra almost wavered. She didn't want it to end like this.

"Mac, can't we at least talk?" she asked hesitantly.

"I'm pretty much all talked out." He slid her a glance as he opened his door. "Besides, I think you said all there was to say."

He hoisted her luggage from the truck bed and walked her to the terminal. A metallic voice was announcing her flight by the time they'd purchased her ticket and reached the gate.

"Well . . ." Her voice caught on a wave of regret. "I guess this is goodbye."

He looked away. This was so stupid. So damn stupid. He didn't know if he was angrier at her or himself. They should be making plans, not saying goodbye. "Not just yet," he decided. "I've got one more thing to say to you."

Her eyes widened. "I thought—"

"I'm damn tired of you thinking all the time." He pulled her into his arms. "Just let me tell you this."

But he didn't say a word. He fused his mouth to hers in a hot, searing kiss. He wanted her to feel his love and his need. And he wanted her to remember, always, that this was special, this was something that only happened once in a lifetime. He felt a rush of satisfaction when her arms curved around his neck and she pulled him closer.

Her eyes were dazed and disappointed when he pulled away from her. Good. That's exactly what he wanted.

"Think about *that* while you're doing all your thinking," he told her, forcing himself to let her go. "And when you've finally figured out that what we feel is more important than knowing whether or not I keep my socks in pairs or you roll the toilet paper from the back or the front, give me a call."

He didn't look back when he walked away.

Eleven

Bridgett was waiting for her when Kendra stepped through the front door of her apartment. No, *waiting* wasn't the right word, she decided wearily as she looked into her sister's surprised blue eyes. *Caught* fit better.

"What are you doing here?" Bridgett's voice was as shaky as Kendra's battered emotions. "I thought you weren't due back till tomorrow."

Kendra dropped her luggage on the softly patterned living-room sofa and followed the pieces with her body. "I had a change of plans." She rubbed her temples to dislodge the headache building there. "What are *you* doing here?" But the question was moot. She could see the boxes Bridgett had stacked near the door.

"You said I could have some of the pots and pans and linens."

Kendra nodded. "Whatever you need." She didn't want to deal with this right now. She only wanted . . . she only wanted Mac. She wanted his arms and his kisses and his cocky grin and—Damn him. She was feeling so much pain, she didn't know which hurt worse—her head, from all the thinking she'd done, or her heart, from missing him.

"What's the matter with you?"

Kendra looked up to see a blurred Bridgett standing across the room.

"Oh, damn." Bridgett's tone was strained. "I was afraid you'd pull a guilt trip on me."

Kendra shook her head dazedly. "What are you talking about?"

"It's not going to work, you know. Crying isn't going to make me change my mind."

Kendra wiped at the tears she hadn't realized were falling. "I'm not trying to get you to change your mind. I'm tired of trying to get you to change your mind."

Is that how Mac had felt? she wondered. Had he gotten tired of trying to change her mind? Her heart throbbed at the thought. Call him, he'd said. She wanted to, just to hear his low, gentle voice. But—

"Kendra?"

She looked back at her sister.

"I don't want you to be upset. Okay?"

Upset? She was dying in bits and pieces. She rubbed her temples again and focused on Bridgett. "Maybe I wouldn't be if I understood what was happening. One day everything was rocking along like clockwork, and the next day you'd dropped out of college and found an apartment, and you wouldn't even discuss it with me."

"It wouldn't have done any good."

"Excuse me?"

Bridgett shoved a lock of thick brown hair away from her exquisite face. "We might as well get this over with, I guess."

Kendra sat up and really looked at her sister, noticing that the set of her jaw didn't look so much like hostility as it did determination. And she looked a little thinner. A little paler. "Are you in some kind of trouble, Bridgett?"

That brought an exasperated laugh. "No."

Relief was Kendra's first emotion. Confusion was the next. "Then what are you so afraid of telling me?"

"I'm not afraid . . . exactly. I just don't want to . . . it's just that—" She heaved a sigh and squared her shoulders. "I want my own life. I want to do what I want and not have to feel guilty all the time because I can't be what you want me to be."

Kendra felt as if she'd had the breath knocked out of her. "What I want you to be? I only want you to be happy, Bridgett. That's all I've ever wanted."

"No. You want me to be some—some mega-genius or something." Her eyes filmed with tears. "But I want something else, Kendra." She lifted her chin. "I want to be an actress."

"An actress!"

Bridgett's chin went higher. "I knew you'd take it like that."

"I'm just . . ." She groped for the right words. "I'm just so surprised." That was the understatement of the century. She was stunned. "Why didn't you tell me?"

"How could I?" Bridgett's voice quavered and

tears trickled down her cheeks. "How could I say no thanks to the college education you were knocking yourself out to give me? How could I not try to do what you wanted when you've sacrificed your whole life for me?" The tears were falling so fast, Bridgett couldn't wipe them away.

Kendra pushed herself off the couch and took Bridgett in her arms. "Sacrifice? You thought I was sacrificing my life for you? That's crazy! I've done exactly what I've wanted to do."

"And don't you think I know how hard it's been for you? Always doing for me, always being both mother and father. You're even thinking about giving up your residency, which you love, so you'd have more money to send me to school."

Kendra stiffened. "That's not . . ." But wasn't it? If she were totally honest, wasn't that the source of her dilemma? She loved trauma residency—the constant upheaval, the constant challenge, the euphoric feeling when she pulled someone back from the brink. But private practice would mean so much more security.

"I just hated hurting you when all you've ever done is take care of me," Bridgett continued. "But I have to do this, Kendra. It's all I've ever wanted, and I just have to."

Kendra stroked Bridgett's hair, remembering how Mac had stroked hers when he'd been holding her and comforting her and telling her to let Bridgett find her own way. "If that's what you want, then I guess that's what you have to do. But you don't have to move out. You could stay here and—"

"No, I can't." Bridgett pulled out of her arms. "I

can't keep taking and taking from you. I'm almost twenty years old. It's time for me to stand on my own two feet."

"You have the rest of your life to do that. For now—"

"No." Bridgett's eyes flooded again. "Do you know how much it kills me even to take these stupid pots and pans? I'm so tired of taking. I want to do this on my own. Just once, just once in my life, I want to do something on my own."

The words sounded like an echo of Kendra's own thoughts when she realized how much she'd wanted Mac and had been afraid to reach for him. But the words weren't what struck deepest into Kendra's heart. It was the desperation in Bridgett's tone. She knew that feeling of desperation, that need to be free, if only just once.

"All right, Bridgett," she said, giving her sister the freedom to follow her dreams. "All right."

Bridgett swiped away the tears. "You're not mad at me?"

"Of course not."

And she wasn't, Kendra thought later, afraid Bridgett had left. Amazed, yes. But not mad. She stared around the apartment, trying to absorb her sister's revelations. Bridgett had everything planned. Doing dinner theater, some local television commercials, anything and everything she could find until she could go to New York and take acting lessons. And her job offered flexible enough hours so that she could manage—barely—to support herself while she was doing it all.

Kendra shook her head, not quite able to believe it. How on God's earth could she have lived with

Bridgett all these years, raised her and loved her and shared every spare moment with her and not have had a clue—

Oh, God. A thunderbolt direct from heaven couldn't have hit her with more force. Maybe she hadn't known everything about her sister—not in the way she'd thought—but the fact that Bridgett had different dreams didn't make Kendra love her any less. Bridgett was still Bridgett. The bone and the marrow and the soul that made Bridgett what she was hadn't changed.

And Mac hadn't changed. If he lived in a penthouse or a pigsty, if he had one restaurant or ten or none, didn't mean a thing. It wasn't what he *had* that she'd fallen in love with. It was what he *was*: good and kind and gentle and funny.

And he loved her. He'd said so. But she'd been too stubborn to believe it because she'd been so afraid it couldn't be true, so afraid it wouldn't last.

Well, it was time to follow Bridgett's example and stop being a coward. It was time to stop worrying about yesterday and tomorrow and start living for today. She reached for the phone, but a sudden surge of panic kept her from picking it up. She didn't know whether to laugh or to cry. It was one thing to think brave—another to act it.

What if he'd changed as much as she had in the course of a few hours? What if . . . No. She was being ridiculous. She hadn't changed. She'd just accepted the truth.

She reached for the phone again and got his listing from information. Her heart pounded like a kettledrum when she punched out the number. But he wasn't home.

• • •

He wasn't home the next day either. Or the next two days after that. Kendra put down the receiver in the doctors' lounge after listening to the twelfth unanswered ring and ran her fingers through her hair. Where was he? She glanced at her watch. Where would he be at nine-forty-seven on a Wednesday night? Call me, he'd said. If he'd meant it, why wasn't he home? She looked around the empty lounge and couldn't decide whether to throw an ashtray or sit down and cry. She poured herself a cup of coffee instead.

"Hey, pour one for me too."

Kendra whirled to face the door. "Leslie! What are you doing here?"

Leslie breezed over to the coffee urn and helped herself. "You were supposed to meet me at your apartment an hour ago, remember?"

Kendra frowned. "No."

Leslie rolled her eyes. "We were going to catch a quick bite and then a movie."

A bell rang in the back of Kendra's mind, but only faintly. "I'm sorry. I'd forgotten, I guess. But I couldn't have made it anyway."

Leslie dropped her long slender frame onto the vinyl couch. "I understand it's been a busy night."

"Wild," Kendra clarified. "Two multiples fractures within forty-five minutes, a coronary, and a stabbing. And that doesn't even cover the routine mishaps. I would have called and canceled our plans if I'd remembered."

"No prob. I knew it was something like that

when I called and old prune-face wouldn't put you on the phone."

Kendra sighed at Leslie's rude but accurate description of the admittance clerk. "Her name is Sadie. So why didn't you just page me?"

"*Sadie* said you were tied up in too many knots to be disturbed, so I figured you didn't need your beeper going off. I hung around the apartment for a while and then decided to come on over and see what was up. Oh, Bridgett called while I was there." Leslie grinned. "She sounds happy as a clam."

Kendra tried not to sigh. "Good. I want her to be happy."

Leslie's expression sobered. "I can't tell you how proud I am of you. I know it's been tough."

"Not as tough as it would have been a couple of weeks ago."

"Oh, Lord. You're not going to start waxing eloquent about that man again, are you?"

Kendra shot Leslie a surprised look. "Weren't you the one who said he sounded like the best thing that's ever happened to me? That falling in love with him was the smartest thing I ever did?"

Leslie shrugged. "I may be changing my mind."

"Excuse me? You don't even know him. You don't know—"

The grin on Leslie's face stopped Kendra's tirade. "Just testing."

"Look, I was an idiot once. I don't intend to be again." She glanced at the phone. "If I ever get to talk to him again." Her breathing hitched. "Where could he be? You don't suppose I blew it so completely that he never wants to see me again, do you?" The thought almost made her ill.

"I thought you said he loved you?"

"He does. He— You're testing again, aren't you?"

"Yup. And you passed with flying—"

"Dr. Davis?" Sadie, the admittance clerk, slapped open the lounge door. "Good, You're still here. I need you in the E.R." She glanced at Leslie. "Stat."

"Where's Dr. Rollings?" Kendra asked, but she was already heading toward the door.

"Busy."

Kendra practically had to run to keep up with the clerk. She could feel Leslie hot on her heels, but she didn't have time to wonder about the psychiatrist's presence.

"In here," Sadie said, stopping outside one of the curtained examining areas. "You"—she pointed to Leslie—"stay out."

"But—"

Kendra didn't hear what Leslie was saying. The moment she stepped through the curtain, she froze.

Mac sat on the examining table, holding his forehead.

"What—?" Her voice caught in her throat, right next to her heart. "Mac, what happened?" She rushed to him, reaching toward his brow with a trembling hand.

He looked up at her, clear-eyed and steady. "They took my stitches out," he said testily. His expression was so disgruntled, she might have laughed if she weren't so relieved. "It's a hell of a deal when a man can't see a woman without having surgery first."

She lowered her hand. Her heart started beating again. "You waited until today to have your stitches out? Mac, didn't the doctor tell you—"

"Don't start with me, Kendra." His eyes dared her to say a word. "I've had about all I can take for one day, what with Sadie refusing to let me in here unless it was some kind of emergency, and Leslie convincing her my stitches were it."

Kendra knew her mouth was hanging open. "Leslie and Sadie—" She shook her head, unable to fight the smile that was spreading from her heart to her mouth. He was so cute when he pouted. And, oh, God, she was so happy to see him.

"I don't want to talk about them either."

She nodded in agreement. She only wanted to talk about him, and her, and the future they were going to share. Whenever and wherever he—

"Now, listen up," he said, lifting a long, narrow cannister from beside him on the table. He slid a roll of papers out and spread them on the table. "These are the blueprints for my new restaurant. I figure I can build it in St. Louis just as well as I can build it anywhere else."

She stared at the prints.

"It'll take six to eight months to complete, once I've settled on the location." He glanced at her as if to ensure she was following him. She was. And she wasn't sure, but she thought she was going to cry.

"And I guess you'll be spending a lot of time here, keeping an eye on the construction and—"

"And if you haven't figured out by then that we should be getting married, you've got no business tending to other people's injuries, because your own head isn't screwed on straight."

"Oh, I don't think it will take me nearly that long," she said softly.

"I love you, dammit, and you—" His gaze flew to hers. "What did you day?"

"I think four weeks is about all the time I'll need to plan a wedding."

It tickled her to see his mouth fall open. "Four . . . ?"

"If you'd stop talking for about two minutes and put your mouth to better use, you might be able to get it down to three."

He probably could have gotten it down to two. He kissed her until she was weak and hot and dizzy and all she could do was cling to him and tell him how much she loved him. Over and over and over again.

"I like hearing you say that," he said, nipping at her neck.

"I love you," she repeated dutifully.

He pulled her closer. "Now that we're officially engaged, do you think maybe it would be okay if you took me back to your place?"

She grinned. "Why, Mr. O'Conner, are you suggesting—"

"No, ma'am. I only want to make some weddin' plans." He tried to look properly serious. "I think you should ask Sugar to be your maid of honor."

Kendra's eyes widened. "The waitress at the lodge?"

"Well, sure. If it weren't for her, you might never have figured out what a really swell hunk I am."

"Regardless. Leslie's going to be my maid of honor."

He slung his arm across her shoulder and nudged her toward the curtain. "I know. I already promised her that—and that she could be godparent to our first-born child."

"You and Leslie talked about this?"

His dimples played hide-and-seek in his cheeks. "How do you think I convinced her to go to bat for me against Sadie?"

"Well!" She tried to sound miffed. "Don't you think you were a little ahead of yourself? How did you know I'd be ready to talk marriage?"

He grinned his cocky grin. "Hope, darlin'. Certain hope."

THE EDITOR'S CORNER

Next month LOVESWEPT brings you spirited heroines and to-die-for heroes in stories that explore romance in all its forms—sensuous, sweet, heartwarming, and funny. And the title of each novel is so deliciously compelling, you won't know which one to read first.

There's no better way to describe Gavin Magadan than as a **LEAN MEAN LOVING MACHINE,** LOVESWEPT #546, by Sandra Chastain, for in his boots and tight jeans he is one dangerously handsome hunk. And Stacy Lanham has made a bet to vamp him! How can she play the seducer when she's much better at replacing spark plugs than setting off sparks? Gavin shows her the way, though, when he lets himself be charmed by the lady whose lips he yearns to kiss. Sandra has created a winner with this enthralling story.

In **SLOW BURN,** LOVESWEPT #547, by Cindy Gerard, passion heats to a boiling point between Joanna Taylor and Adam Dursky. When he takes on the job of handyman in her lodge, she's drawn to a loneliness in him that echoes her own, and she longs for his strong embrace with a fierce desire. Can a redheaded rebel who's given up on love heal the pain of a tough renegade? The intensity of Cindy's writing makes this a richly emotional tale you'll long remember.

In Linda Jenkins's newest LOVESWEPT, #548, Sam Wonder *is* **MR. WONDERFUL,** a heart-stopping combination of muscles and cool sophistication. But he's furious when Trina Bartok shows up at his Ozarks resort, convinced she's just the latest candidate in his father's endless matchmaking. Still, he can't deny the sensual current that crackles between them, and when Trina makes it clear she's there only for a temporary job, he resolves to make her a permanent part of his life. Be sure not to miss this treat from Linda.

Judy Gill's offering for the month, **SUMMER LOVER,** LOVESWEPT #549, will have you thinking summer may be the most romantic season of all—although romance is the furthest thing from Donna Mailer's mind when she goes to Gray Kincaid's office to refuse his offer to buy her uncle's failing campground business. After all, the Kincaid family nearly ruined her life. But Gray's passionate persuasion soon has her sweetly surrendering amid tangled sheets. Judy's handling of this story is nothing less than superb.

Most LOVESWEPTs end with the hero and heroine happily deciding to marry, but Olivia Rupprecht, who has quickly developed a reputation for daring to be different, begins **I DO!,** #550, with Sol Standish in the Middle East and Mariah Garnett in the Midwest exchanging wedding vows through the telephone—and that's before they ever lay eyes on each other. When they finally come face-to-face, will their innocent love survive the test of harsh reality? Olivia will take your breath away with this original and stunning romance.

INTIMATE VIEW by Diane Pershing, LOVESWEPT #551, will send you flying in a whirlwind of exquisite sensation. Ben Kane certainly feels that way when he glimpses a goddess rising naked from the ocean. He resented being in a small California town to run a cable franchise until he sees Nell Pritchard and she fires his blood—enough to make him risk the danger of pursuing the solitary spitfire whose sanctuary he's invaded. Diane's second LOVE-SWEPT proves she's one of the finest newcomers to the genre.

On sale this month from FANFARE are three marvelous novels. The historical romance **HEATHER AND VELVET** showcases the exciting talent of a rising star—Teresa Medeiros. Her marvelous touch for creating memorable characters and her exquisite feel for portraying passion and emotion shine in this grand adventure of love between a bookish orphan and a notorious highwayman known as the Dreadful Scot Bandit. Ranging from the storm-swept English countryside to the wild moors of Scotland, **HEATHER AND VELVET** has garnered the following praise from *New York Times* bestselling author Amanda Quick: "A terrific tale full of larger-than-life characters and thrilling romance." Teresa Medeiros—a name to watch for.

Lush, dramatic, and poignant, **LADY HELLFIRE,** by Suzanne Robinson, is an immensely thrilling historical romance. Its hero, Alexis de Granville, Marquess of Richfield, is a cold-blooded rogue whose tragic—and possibly violent—past has hardened his heart to love . . . until he melts at the fiery touch of Kate Grey's sensual embrace.

Anna Eberhardt, whose short romances have been published under the pseudonym Tiffany White, has been nominated for *Romantic Times*'s Career Achievement award for Most Sensual Romance in a series. Now she delivers **WHISPERED HEAT,** a compelling contemporary novel of love lost, then regained. When Slader Reems is freed after five years of being wrongly imprisoned, he sets out to reclaim everything that was taken from him—including Lissa Jamison.

Also on sale this month, in the Doubleday hardcover edition, is **LIGHTNING,** by critically acclaimed Patricia Potter. During the Civil War, nobody was a better Confederate blockade runner than Englishman Adrian Cabot, but Lauren Bradley swore to stop him. Together they would be swept into passion's treacherous sea, tasting deeply of ecstasy and the danger of war.

Happy reading!

With warmest wishes,

Nita Taublib
Associate Publisher
LOVESWEPT and FANFARE

FANFARE

Rosanne Bittner

_____ 28599-8 EMBERS OF THE HEART . $4.50/5.50 in Canada
_____ 29033-9 IN THE SHADOW OF THE MOUNTAINS
$5.50/6.99 in Canada
_____ 28319-7 MONTANA WOMAN .... $4.50/5.50 in Canada
_____ 29014-2 SONG OF THE WOLF .... $4.99/5.99 in Canada

Deborah Smith

_____ 28759-1 THE BELOVED WOMAN .. $4.50/ 5.50 in Canada
_____ 29092-4 FOLLOW THE SUN .... $4.99/ 5.99 in Canada
_____ 29107-6 MIRACLE .... $4.50/ 5.50 in Canada

Tami Hoag

_____ 29053-3 MAGIC .... $3.99/4.99 in Canada

Dianne Edouard and Sandra Ware

_____ 28929-2 MORTAL SINS .... $4.99/5.99 in Canada

Kay Hooper

_____ 29256-0 THE MATCHMAKER, ... $4.50/5.50 in Canada
_____ 28953-5 STAR-CROSSED LOVERS .. $4.50/5.50 in Canada

Virginia Lynn

_____ 29257-9 CUTTER'S WOMAN, ... $4.50/4.50 in Canada
_____ 28622-6 RIVER'S DREAM, ... $3.95/4.95 in Canada

Patricia Potter

_____ 29071-1 LAWLESS .... $4.99/ 5.99 in Canada
_____ 29069-X RAINBOW .... $4.99/ 5.99 in Canada

Ask for these titles at your bookstore or use this page to order.
Please send me the books I have checked above. I am enclosing $ _____ (please add
$2.50 to cover postage and handling). Send check or money order, no cash or C. O. D.'s
please.

Mr./ Ms. _____

Address _____

City/ State/ Zip _____
Send order to: Bantam Books, Dept. FN, 414 East Golf Road, Des Plaines, IL 60016
Please allow four to six weeks for delivery.
Prices and availablity subject to change without notice.   FN 17 - 4/92

FANFARE

Sandra Brown

- [ ] 28951-9 TEXAS! LUCKY ....$4.50/$5.50 in Canada
- [ ] 28990-X TEXAS! CHASE ....$4.99/$5.99 in Canada
- [ ] 29500-4 TEXAS! SAGE ....$4.99/$5.99 in Canada
- [ ] 29085-1 22 INDIGO PLACE ....$4.50/$5.50 in Canada

Amanda Quick

- [ ] 28594-7 SURRENDER ....$4.50/$5.50 in Canada
- [ ] 28932-2 SCANDAL ....$4.95/$5.95 in Canada
- [ ] 28354-5 SEDUCTION ....$4.99/$5.99 in Canada
- [ ] 29325-7 RENDEZVOUS ....$4.99/$5.99 in Canada

Deborah Smith

- [ ] 28759-1 THE BELOVED WOMAN ....$4.50/$5.50 in Canada
- [ ] 29092-4 FOLLOW THE SUN ....$4.99/$5.99 in Canada
- [ ] 29107-6 MIRACLE ....$4.50/$5.50 in Canada

Iris Johansen

- [ ] 28855-5 THE WIND DANCER ....$4.95/$5.95 in Canada
- [ ] 29032-0 STORM WINDS ....$4.99/$5.99 in Canada
- [ ] 29244-7 REAP THE WIND ....$4.99/$5.99 in Canada

Available at your local bookstore or use this page to order.

Send to: Bantam Books, Dept. FN 18
414 East Golf Road
Des Plaines, IL 60016

Please send me the items I have checked above. I am enclosing
$_____ (please add $2.50 to cover postage and handling). Send
check or money order, no cash or C.O.D.'s, please.

Mr./Ms._____

Address_____

City/State_____Zip_____

Please allow four to six weeks for delivery.

Prices and availability subject to change without notice.   FN 18 1/92